SHIPWRECKED ON A TRAFFIC ISLAND

SHIPWRECKED ON
A TRAFFIC ISLAND

AND OTHER PREVIOUSLY UNTRANSLATED GEMS

COLETTE

Translated by Zack Rogow and Renée Morel

excelsior editions
State University of New York Press
Albany, New York

Published by State University of New York Press, Albany

Excelsior Editions is an imprint of State University of New York Press

For information, contact State University of New York Press, Albany, NY
www.sunypress.edu

Production, Jenn Bennett
Marketing, Fran Keneston

Library of Congress Cataloging-in-Publication Data

Colette, 1873–1954.
  [Works. Selections. English]
  Shipwrecked on a traffic island : and other previously untranslated gems / Colette ; translated by Zack Rogow and Renée Morel.
    pages cm. — (Excelsior editions)
  Collection of translated fiction, personal essays, articles, columns and talks.
  ISBN 978-1-4384-5443-6 (hardcover : alk. paper)
  I. Rogow, Zack, translator. II. Morel, Renée, translator. III. Title.

  PQ2605.O28A2 2014
  848'.91209—dc23   2014008968

10 9 8 7 6 5 4 3 2 1

Contents

Acknowledgments

The translators wish to thank the Arts and Letters Foundation for a generous donation to help support their work.

Zack Rogow thanks the Brown Foundation Fellows program at the Museum of Fine Arts, Houston, for a residency at the Dora Maar House in Ménerbes, France, that provided essential time to complete the first draft of these translations.

The translators extend their thanks to Anne de Jouvenel, Foulques de Jouvenel, and Hugues de Jouvenel, for their cooperation in making these texts available to English-speaking readers.

We also wish to thank Frédéric Maget, president of the Société des amis de Colette (Society of Friends of Colette) for his help in choosing, locating, and granting permission for the reprinting of these texts, and for his tireless efforts to keep Colette's literary legacy alive.

The translators wish to thank the following publications for printing sections of this book:

"Loves," *Chicago Quarterly Review*; "The Young Poet," *The MacGuffin*; "The Eyes of the Dragonfly," *Orion*; "Gone Fishin'," *Catamaran Literary Reader*; "Portrait of the Poet Léon-Paul Fargue," *Kestrel*; "Jealousy," *Ploughshares*; selections from Colette's advice column, *The Believer* blog; "Shipwrecked on a Traffic Island," "Ways of Writing," *Yale Review*; "From Both Sides of the Curtain," *American Theatre*; "Conversation in the Metro" and "Divine" in *Hanging Loose*.

Introduction

Shipwrecked on a Traffic Island is the first new work by Colette to appear in English in half a century. This collection of her fiction, personal essays, articles, and talks includes some of her best writing. It shows the whole range of Colette's gifts as an author: her deep wisdom about every age of human life, her skill as a storyteller, her wry humor, her persuasive powers, and her foresight as a social critic. We have meticulously combed through journals and past editions of Colette's work to cull the best pieces that have never before been translated into English. The selections include an advice column that Colette wrote for the French women's magazine *Marie Claire*, and her suggestions for the lovelorn remain to this day amazingly savvy and original.

This collection shows sides of Colette that have won her many English-language followers, such as her insight into how gender roles were changing in her time. It also showcases facets of her writing that are less often celebrated, including her moving journalism written during the two world wars, and her memories of her career as an actor and playwright.

Colette is best known as the author of the classic novels *Gigi* and *Cheri*, both made into popular movies about the world of French courtesans. She visits that demi-monde in this book as well, but she also writes about an enormous variety of other topics, from French wines and perfumes to her friendships with Marcel Proust and Maurice Chevalier. Colette also displays in this collection her uncanny insight into the curious habits of cats and dogs and other living creatures.

We hope that this collection surprises and delights Colette's English-speaking fans and admirers with the range of her interests as a writer, even if they are already familiar with her profundity as a human being.

Zack Rogow and Renée Morel, San Francisco, 2014

Stories Imagined and Real

Conversation in the Metro

This is one of Colette's many writings about the performing arts. For several years she made her living as a mime and actor. An amusing part of this "conversation" is that the listener only hears one side of the dialogue. The Oberkampf metro station is located on the Right Bank of Paris in the 11th Arrondissement, and was then in a district populated by workers and artisans. This story was first published in the newspaper *Le Matin* on April 30, 1914.

They've just run into one another on a train. They are both young, made-up, poor, pretty, all skin and bones. They have the self-assurance that comes less from innate impudence than from the habit of living in public since they were born: first in the streets, then on stage in variety shows. One speaks very loudly, too loudly. I can hardly hear the responses of the other, whose voice is hoarse and weak.

"Me? In the new show, I'm playing a chauffeur, a misuse of taxpayers' funds, and an iris. What about you?"

"—"

"Oh, I see. Something like a gas lamp in the distance. Practically nothing, in other words. What really bugs me is the hairstyles for the extras these past few years. They say it's because of those Russian ballets."

"—"

"I mean that before, for the extras, it was usually wigs, or shepherdess hats, or a fall of hair; but now, it's these monuments they stick on our heads, or these things with spangles and fake jewels, or imitation fur hats, and helmets worse than firemen wear. The migraines they give me! And I'm not the only one. Not to mention the heat. . . ."

"—?"

"Yeah, they're cooking us with all that heat where I am, and the concierge, who sells drinks, she doesn't let a thing get past her that you don't buy from her. Not everybody is a star who can treat themselves to water with mint syrup at four sous a glass. We all wanted to buy stuff from outside, but the old bitch said she'd stop any 'disguised packages' from getting through, that's what she called them. Me, I drink when I get home to my estate, y'know?"

"—?"

"Yeah, we worked it out so it's cheaper. Hundred forty francs a year, for a room with a toilet and sink, that's not bad, though you would think at that price it wouldn't rain in your room. So the guy who wrote the Christmas show, who came by once, you know, like a tourist, he says, 'You live in a historic home, my children, a relic of the old Montmartre, a true wonder!' A wonder like that, he wouldn't pay three francs to put in his play. Long story short, I'm all alone in the wonder. Alice—she's in the hospital."

"—?"

"Luckily, no, it's not contagious. That's funny, you know! She was six months pregnant, but she kept working. You remember, she was playing a naked woman in the orgy? When she started to show a little, she figured they would *show* her politely to the door, which is only fair, but it turned out the director had a heart and he kept her in the show. He changed her role in the orgy, they moved her farther back and put her in a big red veil from the waist down, and since she's got a nice bust, she could've continued like that till her delivery, if she hadn't fallen, and fallen bad, on our stairs, see. She's in the hospital. Doesn't look good."

"—?"

"Oh, yeah, you should go, that would be really nice of you. If you'd seen her, the poor kid, when they took her away . . . and the dog, that she'd found a month before, who didn't know a soul but her, he clamped so tight to her when they carried her downstairs—the thing was crying like a human being. I never saw him again, that dog. You getting off at the next one?"

"—?"

"No, I'm going as far as Oberkampf. Yeah, sure, drop by sometime. And about the kid, if you want to see her again, don't wait too long."

Divine

This short story was first published in a book where twenty-six authors each wrote a story about a character whose name started with one letter of the alphabet, from A to Z. A different artist illustrated each one of the texts. The book is entitled *D'Ariane à Zoé, Alphabet gallant et sentimental agrémenté de vers, de proses et de lithographies par 26 écrivains et autant d'artistes*, published by Librairie de France in 1930. The Venus of Cyrene is a classic sculpture not found until 1912 in Libya, a Roman copy of a Hellenistic statue thought to be by Praxiteles. It depicts Venus rising from the sea.

"Stop, already!" yells Divine, without opening the door. "You trying to break my doorbell? Who's ringing, anyway?"

A voice that seems to pierce through miles of fog, a voice husky with the dawn, sweet and male like those pastoral voices in the meadows that wake the sleepy cows, pearly with dew, that voice answers: "It's the milk."

"Of course it's the milk! Just leave it at the corner of the doorway. I'll get it in a second!"

She adjusts, before opening the door, the belt of her pajamas, and wiggles her feet into her slippers. Then she changes her mind and walks into the kitchen to turn down the burners with their flames of blue sepals just touching the bottom of a small copper laundry pot full of water; she opens a transom that lets in the musty air of a courtyard, its odor of sprouted potatoes, coffee, and a cellar without wine; she takes in from the windowsill a stick of butter hardened by the cold.

When she comes back to open the door a crack, "The Milk" is still there. He has beautiful, curly blond hair, cut in a crest in the Parisian style; bright eyes; and purplish hands.

"Good morning, Mademoiselle Divine."

"Never in hurry, huh? What are you waiting for, standing here on my doormat?"

"A ticket to the Sunday matinee."

"Again?"

The eyes of "The Milk" wander over Divine, searching downwards for a flash of leg, higher up for a rising orb.

"Beat it! We'll see about that. C'mon, beat it! And your customers, you don't care a lick whether they get any breakfast?"

"I've got one of the two new trucks," answers "The Milk." "That way, I make good time. I'm bringing you six eggs laid just today, to thank you for the ticket from the other Sunday. You can gulp them right down."

"Now that's a rare treat," says Divine without irony.

"The Milk," showing off, shrugs his shoulders: "Hey, what is that to us? Seven hundred white chickens, without a mark on them! If my parents listened to me, we'd double the number. So, Mademoiselle Divine, the Sunday matinee?"

"We'll see. Get going, now, the water for my coffee is boiling over!"

When the door closes, Divine listens to the steps of "The Milk" on the stairs, and the bottles clanking like cowbells. As if reassured, she takes off her pajamas and for five minutes she "runs through her exercise drills," following the peremptory advice of her friends.

At the Casino de Paris, Divine practices the profession of being a naked woman. The beauty of her body so strictly adheres to the norms of antiquity that it seems at first glance ordinary. As for her head, it resembles a brown-haired boy's, with a graceful and empty youth about it, and as for the rest, it's like the Venus of Cyrene. That is to say that on an ample chest, her two conical breasts tremble neither when Divine laughs nor when she runs, and that from the nape of her neck to the small of her back the concave and living imprint of a peaceful snake nonchalantly undulates. Her long thighs, her knees with their oval caps, rest on a solid ankle, not very high, that has for its base a wide foot with toes that unfold gracefully. Under the skin of her calf—downy, rough, and cold like peaches grown in the wind—a powerful muscle, discreet, vaguely traces the shape of a heart.

Village blood nourishes Divine's depilated flesh. A uniform amber tone covers her, a bit greenish under the stage lights. When her cousin Betty, a performer with the Folies Bergère, came to see her in her village in a five-horsepower car and they bathed together in the stream, these two young women did not waste time in idle conversation.

"What are you going to do, Ludivine?"

"Next month I'm starting at the factory of United Jams."

"You start earning right off the bat?"

"Yeah. Fifteen francs to start out."

"What if I could find you something in Paris where you'd earn forty francs right off the bat?"

"Then I'd go to Paris."

"Your mother wouldn't say anything against it?"

"Not if it were written in a contract."

On the stage of the Casino, every evening at nine-thirty, a giant clam made out of painted cardboard yawns and reveals Divine, naked, a pearl lying among pearls. She stands up, opens her arms, and slowly inhales. Lipstick that is almost black thickens the arc of her motionless mouth and her eyes receive without blinking, wide open like the eyes of a blind man, a terrible punishment of light.

Later she reappears, naked, carried on the ravishing arms of a naked man. We see her again upside down with the violet coloring of a bottle of wine turned upside down, in the throes of The Orgy.

Walking from the stage to the dressing room that she shares with Sylvana the blond and Maryse the mulatto, Divine receives homages. In three months, she has achieved a small portion of fame. Along the way she never opens her crepon kimono even a bit, and she only extends one finger to her admirers.

"I don't like those guys with the warm hands," she confides to Sylvana.

Proud and secretive, Divine says no more. And all that she locks in her heart—rural wisdom, the poetry of the exile, respect for the fruits of the earth—it all turns toward the young man from the pastures with the icy hands, joyful as dawn, patient, sweet, scented like a blond heifer—toward "The Milk."

The Woman Who Sings

This is a rare short story where Colette takes on the persona of a male narrator. Or does she? Colette mentions in passing the devastating fire in the crowded charity bazaar on the rue Jean-Goujon that took place on May 4, 1897. There was a famous scramble where everyone tried to rush out to avoid succumbing to the fire. One hundred and seventeen died, many of them from the Paris elite. This story originally appeared in Colette's book *Les Vrilles de la vigne* in a later edition that she published in 1934.

The woman who was about to sing headed for the piano, and right away I turned ferocious, feeling the concentrated and motionless revolt of a prisoner. While she cleaved her way through a sea of skirts belonging to seated women, her dress stuck to her knees like muddy ripples, and I wished that she would faint, die, or even simultaneously rip her four garters. She still had several meters to cross: thirty seconds, room enough for a cataclysm. But she strode serenely over a few feet in patent leather, frayed the lace of a flounce, muttered "Excuse me," greeted us, and smiled, her hand already on the dark Brazilian rosewood of the Pleyel with its reflections like the Seine at night. I began to feel pain.

I noticed, across the dancing fog that forms a halo around the chandeliers when the evening dims, the curved back of my heavy-set friend Maugis, his bent arm defending his full glass against stray elbows. I realized I hated him for having managed to get to the buffet table, while I wasted away, trapped, seated sideways on the gilded caning of a fragile chair.

With insolent coldness, I stared fixedly at the lady who was about to sing, and I held in a sneer of diabolical joy, finding her even uglier than I had hoped.

Caparisoned in metallic white satin, she held her head high, topped with a helmet of unnatural, violently blond hair. All the arrogance of women who are too short blazed in her hard eyes, where there was much blue and not enough black. Her protruding cheekbones, her nose restless and open, her chin solid and ready to squeal, all that created the impression of a pug-nosed snout. Before she could say a word I wanted to call out to that face, "Here, sooey!"

And her mouth! Her mouth! With disdain I focused my glance on her uneven lips, carved by an errant penknife. I calculated the vast opening they would soon unveil, the quality of the sounds that cavern would moo. What a trapdoor she had! My ears burned in anticipation, and I clamped my jaws shut.

The woman who was about to sing planted herself immodestly, directly facing the audience, straightened her posture in her stiff corset, making the apples of her bust jut out. She breathed deeply, coughed, and cleared her throat in the disgusting manner of great performers.

In the anxious silence where the perfumed armatures of fans creaked like minuscule punkas, the piano began its prelude. And suddenly a sharp note, a vibrant cry pierced right to my brain, bristled the skin of my spine: the woman was singing. After this first cry, which sprang from the very depths of her chest, came the languor of a phrase, nuanced by the most velvet of mezzos, the fullest, the most tangible I'd ever heard. Transfixed, I lifted my glance toward the woman who was singing. She had definitely grown taller than a mere instant ago. With her wide eyes open and blind, she was contemplating something invisible that her entire body was hurtling toward, out of her armor of white satin. The blue of her eyes had darkened and her hair, dyed or not, adorned her with a firm flame, rising straight up. Her large and generous mouth opened and I saw burning notes fly from it, some like golden bubbles, others like pure round roses. Trills shone like a rustling stream, like a lithe snake; slow vocalizations caressed me, a cool hand lingering. Unforgettable voice! Fascinated, I began to contemplate that large mouth, its lips painted and rolling over wide teeth, that golden door of sound, jewel case of a thousand gems. Pink blood colored her Kalmuk cheekbones, her shoulders filled with a quick breath, her throat thrust forward in a gesture of offering. At the foot of that bust held in passionate immobility, two expressive hands twisted their naked fingers. Only her eyes, almost black, soared over us, blind and serene.

"Love!" sang the voice. And I saw that mouth, misshapen, moist, and crimson, close on the word while sketching the image of a kiss. A desire so sudden and insane grabbed me that my eyelids moistened with nervous tears. The marvelous voice trembled, as if choked by a tide of blood, and the thick lashes of the woman who was singing fluttered, just once. I wanted to drink that voice from its source, to feel it spring from the polished stones of her teeth, to dam its flow just for one minute with my own lips, to hear it, see it leap, a free torrent, and bloom into a long harmonious sheet that I would crack with a caress. To be the lover of that woman transfigured by her voice—and of that voice! Sequestered for me—only for me!—that voice more moving than the most secret caress, and that woman's second face, her maddening and demure mask of a nymph drunk on dreams!

Just when I was succumbing to these delights, the woman who was singing fell silent. My cry—like that of a man falling—was lost in a polite tumult of applause, in the "wows" that mean *bravo* in the language of salons. The woman who sang leaned forward to thank them, unfurling a smile between her and us, a flutter of her eyelids that separated her from the world. She took the pianist's arm and attempted to arrive at the doorway; her train of trampled, bruised satin hindered her steps. Gods! was I going to lose her? Already a corner of her white armor was all I could see. I threw myself forward savagely, with a devastating fury like certain "survivors" of the bazaar at the rue Jean-Goujon.

Finally, finally, I reached her, when she was next to the buffet table, fortunate isle, laden with fruits and flowers, scintillating with crystal and spangling wines.

She held out her hand, and my trembling hands rushed to offer her a full champagne flute. But she bluntly refused, reaching for a bottle of Bordeaux: "Thank you, monsieur, but champagne doesn't agree with me, especially just after I sing. It goes right to my legs. Especially since these kind ladies and gentlemen insist on my singing *The Life and Love of a Woman,* can you imagine?" And her large mouth—an ogre's cave where a magic bird nests—puckered against fine crystal which she could have smashed to pieces with a smile.

I didn't feel even a drop of sadness, and no anger. All I remembered was: she was going to sing again. I waited, respectfully, for her to empty another glass of the Bordeaux, for her to wipe, with a gesture like scouring a pot, the wings of her nostrils, the deplorable corners of her lips, to air out her damp armpits, to flatten out her stomach with a sharp slap, and to steady on her forehead the false front of her peroxide hair.

I waited, resigned, battered, but full of hope, for the miracle of her voice to give her back to me.

Jealousy

Colette published this exploration of jealousy around the time she separated from her lover Missy, the Marquise de Belbeuf (1862–1945). It was first printed on February 22, 1912, in *Le Matin*, a newspaper edited by her soon-to-be second husband, Henri de Jouvenel (1876–1935).

I'm chewing on a sprig of bitter herb that makes my saliva taste of boxwood and turpentine. The wind dries the water of the waves from my arms, from my cheek; and having twisted, all along the footpath, stems of broom that brushed my hands, my fingers remain acrid and green. I am carrying in me, on me, the aroma and the taste, the salt and bitterness of my jealousy.

I fled from you, along the path of gorse that cards my dress. I've reached a dry shelter that you don't know, a sonorous lookout of rock. A swirling wind inhabits it and seems always to be imprisoned here. Below me, amid long, tapering reefs, the sea, ashen and green like the gray leaves of olive trees, torments itself and fizzes with the violence of a dammed-up stream.

It's a beautiful spot for a refuge. In the distance I can see our house, clothed in dark and varnished ivy. You're back there. You read, your forehead between your two fists, like a schoolboy. Or maybe you're sleeping, because sleep surprises you capriciously in the middle of the day and throws you down, no matter where you are, for brief and deep rests.

I watch out for you carefully, from the heights of my jagged tower. If you open the door, the flash of the glass will warn me—but won't I first see your greyhound whirling on the grass, quick and white as a pigeon?

You won't come. I have time to calm myself. For a long time I chew the sprig of bitter herb that has exactly the corrosive and acrid taste of my pain—I'm jealous.

God keep me from looking for help from you! The reassuring word, the persuasive caress, and the promises. My poor lover, beyond reproach, you would lavish them on me in vain. You still believe, oh simple one, that fidelity begets trust. You don't know. You can't conceive of jealousy without hope—the hope of reconquering a belonging that is vied for or surreptitiously stolen from you. It is so innocent, your masculine jealousy, and so active! It expends its energy in the stern attentions of a wronged property owner, so it almost takes on the austere pleasure of work. You imagine, you see obstinately behind me the shadow of a man—that's all. I envy you.

Alone, you stand alone before me, on the ravaged field of the sea. Alone, between me and the choppy waves, the color of absinthe. Your first love, and your earliest memory, the last face you kissed before mine, I forget them, I shove them aside carelessly, impatiently. Alone, it's alone that I contemplate you here, that I beg you here—and I curse you alone.

If you could understand . . . I'm jealous. It happened to me. I don't know when, I don't know how. I remember one day I came home—you were standing there behind me—and it was as if I'd discovered you, as I quivered with a strange fury that combined the astonishment of possessing you, the sudden foreknowledge that I'd lose you, and the humiliation of belonging to you. It seemed to me that, up till then, I had almost not noticed you.

At that moment, I saw you suddenly—you blocked out all of the window and the sea speckled with islands, I couldn't see anything but you—your shape, slightly inclined, of a man who is going to spring forward and run, your amorous way of inhaling a flower that has too strong an aroma. That's where I started to measure, with a very quiet muttering, the place you held in my life. That's where I wanted, for the first time, to turn you out . . . too late.

Too late! Your tyranny was already in full bloom, scandalously safe. Already you used me royally, sure of finding in me something inexhaustible. Already you were blooming in me like a beautiful province that nourishes all its fruits: I was, depending on the hour, depending on your whim, the mouth, silent and hot; or a fraternal arm; better—I was a friendly and wise voice and advisor. I was everything to you, without effort, without fault, and I didn't even suspect it.

It was that knowledge that made me miserly and jealous. Not that I would want to take back what I give: I couldn't. But I come here to protest and to lament, in the name of an imaginary equity: what I am to you, it is inevitable that you will be that for another. Does she exist? It hardly matters. But I foresee, I prepare, for another, a lover, a love, whose magnificence only I know—a love created in my own image.

I pine to think that one day, you, you whom I fulfill, you will become my equal, when I'm no longer close to you. You will become my equal to dismay another woman with love, or rather to live by her side as I live here, proud, wasted, inexhaustible . . . I'm jealous. When I create you as you will be, you dazzle me. It's as if I took off, to better appraise them, the ornaments I'm wearing: when they shine on you I cry to see them so precious, but I no longer dare to extend my empty hands. May my jewels, dangling from you, at least protect you from my jealousy, which knows neither time nor space!

I distance myself, without the strength to do you harm. I come here, through a path of thorns, I climb as far as this dungeon of rocks where the wind and my worry struggle with a shackled wing between them. There is nothing more in me, below or above me, than the whipped sea, crumbling stone, breathless clouds. This storm of air and water, this jumble of reclining rocks, that is how my inner disorder has been distributed, to your glory—oh, you, who just appeared on the threshold of our house, so small in the distance, clear, tapered, minuscule, and terrifying.

By the Bay of Somme

The Bay of Somme is located in the province of Picardy in Northern France, along the English Channel, with its dramatic tides. It's a popular location for bird-watching and fishing. Hourdel, Le Crotoy, and Saint-Valery are towns in this region. Crécy Forest is one of the largest woods in France. First published in *Les Vrilles de la vigne* in 1908.

This mild landscape, flat and blond—could it be less simple than I thought? There are odd customs here: they fish from vehicles, they hunt in boats. "Bye! The fishing boat's about to go, I hope I'll bring down a nice snipe to roast tonight." Then the hunter leaves, packed into his yellow oilskin, his rifle slung over his shoulder. "Kids, come look! The carts are coming back! Their nets are hanging from the poles just bursting with sand dabs!" Strange, for those who don't know that game ventures over the bay and crosses it, from Hourdel to Le Crotoy, from Le Crotoy to Saint-Valery; strange, for someone who hasn't clambered into one of those carts with huge wheels that take the fishermen along twenty-five kilometers of beaches, to meet the sea.

Stunning weather. We left the children to bake together on the beach. Some roast on the dry sand, others simmer in the saucepans of warm pools. A young mother under a striped beach umbrella deliciously forgets her two kids. Her cheeks warm as she gets drunk on a mystery novel, clothed like her in unbleached holland.

"Mama! Mama, oh, mama!"

Her pudgy little boy, patient and stubborn, waits, shovel in hand, his cheeks dusted with sand like a cake.

"Mama, mama!"

Finally the eyes of the reader rise, sunstruck, and she lets out a weary little bark: "What?"

"Mama, Jeannine drowned."

"What? What are you talking about?"

"Jeannine drowned," repeats the well-behaved, pudgy little boy, stubbornly.

The book goes flying, the folding chair collapses.

"What are you saying, you little snip? Your sister drowned?"

"Uh huh. She was there just a minute ago, and now she's not there anymore. So I think she drowned."

The young mother whirls around like a seagull and is about to scream when she notices the "drowned girl" at the bottom of a huge bowl of sand, where she is digging like a fox-terrier.

"Jojo! Aren't you ashamed to make up stories like that to keep me from reading? No cream puff for you at snack time!"

The well-behaved, pudgy boy opens wide his candid eyes.

"But I didn't do it to bug you, Mama! Jeannine wasn't there anymore, so I thought she'd drowned."

"Lord! He believed it! And that's your only reaction?"

Dismayed, her hands knitted together, she contemplates her pudgy little son from across the abyss that separates a civilized grown-up from a savage child.

My little bulldog has lost his mind. On the trail of sandpipers and ringed plover, he stops, then runs away like mad, loses his breath, dives into the rushes, gets stuck, swims, and then comes back empty-handed but delirious, shaking back and forth an imaginary fleece. And I understand that an obsession has grabbed hold of him and that he now actually believes he's a cocker spaniel on a hunt.

The Nun and the Redfoot Knight gossip with the Harlequin. The Nun inclines her head, then runs, flirtatiously, wanting to be followed, making little cries. The Redfoot Knight, with boots of orange leather, whistles cynically, while the Harlequin, shifty and thin, spies on them.

O, depraved reader, who was hoping for a good old-fashioned, raunchy anecdote, undeceive yourself: I'm just recounting to you the revels of three lovely birds in the swamp.

They have charming names, these birds of the sea and wetlands. Names redolent of *commedia dell'arte*, even Roman heroics—like the sandpiper called the *Chevalier Combattant*, "The Fighting Knight," this warrior of a bygone age, who sports a plastron and bristly ruff, with horns of feathers on his forehead. A vulnerable plastron, harmless horns, but the male of the species is true to his name, since the Fighting Knights kill each other under the peaceful eye of their females, an indifferent harem sitting on the sand, crouched in a ball.

In a little café by the port, fishermen wait for the tide to come in before leaving, the tide that's already slyly tickling keels of the boats that are stuck in the sand at an angle, at the end of the quai. They're the type of fisherman you see everywhere, with clothes made of fabric like tarpaulins, blue knit sweaters, and pug-nosed clogs. The old ones have a closely trimmed beard and a short pipe. They're the current model, popularized by prints and snapshots.

They drink coffee with an easy laugh, and with their bright eyes devoid of thought, they charm us—the landlubbers. One of them is as striking as an actor, neither young nor old, with a woolly fleece of hair and beard, paler than his weather-beaten skin, and the yellowy eyes and pupils of a dreamy nanny goat that almost never blinks.

The tide has risen, the boats dance on the bay at the ends of their moorings, their bellies clink against one other. One by one the fishermen leave, shaking the paw of the handsome guy with the golden eyes: "See yah, Canada." In the end, Canada is left alone in the café, standing, his forehead pressed to the window, his glass of brandy in hand. What's he waiting for? I'm impatient and decide to speak to him:

"Are they going a long way out?"

With a slow gesture, his deep glance indicates the high seas: "Out there. Lots of shrimp right now. Good catch of sand dabs and mackerel and sole. A little of everything."

"So you're not going fishing today?"

The golden pupils turn toward me, slightly haughty:

"Heck, no, lady, I'm no fisherman. I'm here with a photographer who shoots postcards. I'm what they call 'the local color.'"

II

SUNBATHING—"Poucette, you're gonna boil your blood! Come here this instant!" Thus apostrophized from the patio above it, the female bulldog lifts only her monstrous, bronze-colored, Japanese muzzle. Her mouth, split all the way to her nape, half opens in a little pant, short and sustained, a mouth blooming with a curled tongue, pink as a begonia. The rest of her body trails behind her, flattened like a dead frog. She hasn't moved an inch, she's not going to move, she's cooking.

A summer mist bathes the Bay of Somme, filled with a neap tide that barely palpitates, flat as a lake. Retreating behind this moist and blue fog, Saint-Quentin Point seems to flutter and float, diaphanous as a mirage. A beautiful day to live without thinking, wearing only a bathing costume!

My bare foot amorously teases the hot stone of the patio, and I'm entertained by Poucette's stubbornness. She continues her sun cure with a tortured smile. "C'mon, get yourself over here, you dirty mutt!" and I walk down the stairway whose bottom steps sink into the sand that covers them, sand more transient than the waves, this living sand that walks, undulates, forms hollows, flies, and creates on the beach, on a windy day, entire hills that it levels the very next day.

The beach dazzles me and reflects back in my face, under my straw cloche hat with the brim folded down to my shoulders, a rising heat, the sudden breath of an opened oven. Instinctively I screen my cheeks with my spread hands, my head turned aside as if in front of a fireplace burning too ardently. My big toes rummage through the sand to seek under these blond and burning ashes, the salty coolness, the moisture of the last tide.

The noon bell rings at Le Crotoy, and my short shadow gathers at my feet, wearing a mushroom in its hair.

The sweetness of feeling defenseless, and, under the weight of an implacably beautiful day, of hesitating, tottering for a minute, my calves alive with a thousand pins and needles, my back tingling under my blue sweater, and then to slide onto the sand, next to the dog wagging its tongue!

Lying on my stomach, a shroud of sand half covers me. If I budge, a fine stream of powder pours out of the hollow behind my knees, tickles the soles of my feet. With my chin resting on my crossed arms, the edge of my cloche hat made of rushes forms the border of what I can see, and at my leisure I can digress, making myself a dark soul in the shade of a straw hut. Under my nose three lazy sandhoppers jump up, with bodies of transparent gray agate. The heat, the heat . . . Distant buzz of the rising waves or is it the blood in my ears? Delicious and fleeting death, where my thoughts dilate, rise, tremble, and evaporate with the azured vapor that vibrates above the dunes.

AT LOW TIDE—Children and more children. Kids, brats, urchins, pipsqueaks, small fry . . . Slang isn't enough, they're too much! By accident, returning to my little villa, isolated and far away, I fall into that little frog pond, into that warm bowl that the sea fills and exits every day.

Red jerseys, blue jerseys, rolled-up pants, sandals—straw cloche hats, berets, and lace bonnets—buckets, pails, folding chairs, cabins . . . All that, which should be charming, makes me melancholy. First of all, because they're too much! And because of one pretty little girl, round as an apple, chubby-cheeked and golden with sturdy legs, how many Parisian kids become the victims of a faith that's both maternal and routine: "The seaside is so good for the children!" There they are, half-naked, pitiful in their nervous skinniness, bulging knees, thighs like crickets, bellies protruding. Their delicate skin has darkened in one month to a cigar brown. That's it. That's enough. Their parents think they have robust complexions, but they're only dyed. They've kept the rings under their eyes, their hollow cheeks. The corrosive water skins their pitiful calves and riles their sleep every night with fever, and the slightest accident lets loose the laughter or easy tears of nerve-wracked children dipped in dishwater coffee.

Haphazardly they splash around, the boys and girls, they moisten the sand of a "fort," they channel the water of a salty puddle. Two little "lobsters" in red jerseys work side by side, brother and sister with the same burnt blond hair, maybe seven- or eight-year-old twins. Both of them, under a knit hat with a pompom, have the same blue eyes, the same cap of hair cut just above the eyebrows. But no eye would mistake one for the other, and even though they're the same, they don't resemble one another.

I couldn't tell you what makes the little girl a little girl. Her legs awkwardly and femininely a bit knock-kneed? Something, in those thighs just barely showing, flares more softly, and with an involuntary grace? No, it's definitely her gestures that give her away. A little naked arm, imperious, comments on and draws in the air all that she's saying. Her fist turns with a supple flick, a certain mobility in her fingers and shoulders, a flirtatious way of planting her fist at the notch of her future waistline.

For one moment she lets her pail and bucket fall to the ground, she arranges something or other on her head—her arms raised, her back bowed, and her nape inclined, she gracefully anticipates the moment when she'll knot, in that same standing and arched position, the net of her veil in front of the mirror in a bachelor flat.

CRECY FOREST—The first time I inhale this forest, my heart fills. A former self rises, it quivers with a sad cheerfulness, points my ears, with my nostrils wide open to drink in the scents.

The wind dies down under this tent of trees, where the air barely sways, heavy, musky. A soft wave of fragrance guides my steps toward wild strawberries, round as pearls, which ripen here in secret, blacken, tremble, and fall, dissolve slowly in a sweet, raspberried decay whose aroma mingles with a greenish honeysuckle, sticky with honey, and with a round of white mushrooms. They were born this very night, and their heads lift the crackling carpet of leaves and twigs. They are the fragile and matt white of new gloves, pearly, moist as a lamb's nose: their fragrance evokes fresh truffles and tuberoses.

Under cover of this centenary cluster of trees, the somber green darkness knows nothing of sun and birds. The imperious shadows of the oaks and ash trees banish from the ground any trace of grass, flowers, moss, even insects. An echo follows us, unsettling, which mimics the rhythm of our footsteps. We miss ring doves, tit birds, the russet bounding of a squirrel, or the luminous little ass of a rabbit. Here the forest, humanity's enemy, flattens them all.

Right next to my cheek, glued to the trunk of the elm my back is propped against, a handsome and crepuscular butterfly is sleeping. I know its name: lycaena. Shut tight, its wings spread in a leaf shape, it's waiting for its moment. Tonight, when the sun sets, tomorrow, in the soaking dawn, it will open its heavy wings, mottled in buff, gray, and black. It will bloom like a pirouetting dancer, showing its two other, shorter wings, bursting with the red of ripe cherries, striated with black velvet—its garish undersides, petticoats worn for parties and the night, which a neuter cloak, during the day, conceals.

Makeup

Colette owned a beauty salon and makeup business in Paris that she opened in 1932. Interestingly, she added this story in a later edition of *Les Vrilles de la vigne* in 1934, a full twenty-six years after the book first appeared in print.

"At your age, if I had put on face powder and lipstick and mascara, you know what my mother would've said? You think that's pretty, that riot of color? That, that . . . carnival mask, those, those . . . exaggerations that just make you look older?"

My daughter doesn't answer me. Just like her at that age, I waited till my mother had finished her sermon. Only in her silence can I make out a certain insolence, because the eye of a girl, lustrous, lively, squinting between its lashes curved like the thorns of a rosebush, is for the most part indecipherable. It would be enough, anyway, if she were to question my loyalty, if she were to ask me point blank: "D'you really think it's ugly? D'you think *I'm* ugly?"

And then I would lay down my weapons. But she shrewdly keeps silent and lets my tired lecture on how she should show some respect for her adolescent beauty fall into a chill void. I even add, as long as we're on the subject, something about "decorum," and to wrap it all up, I invoke the miracles of nature, corollas, the flesh of fruits, eternal examples—can you picture a rose with makeup, a painted cherry?

But gone are the days when sharp-tongued young women in the provinces secretly dunked their fingers into the flour jar; crushed geranium petals onto their lips; and collected, under a plate licked by a candle flame, a black smoke as black as their shady little souls.

How skillful our daughters are these days! A shaded cheek, more brown than pink, barely perceptible makeup coloring the eyelids bluish, or gray, or a muted green; their eyes sparkling and their mouths bursting with color, they're not afraid of anything. They're much better made-up than their elders. Because a woman between thirty or forty often hesitates: "Will I look thirty or forty? Or twenty-five? Should I call on the colors of flowers or fruits to come to my rescue?" It's the age of attempts, hesitations, mistakes, disarray that sends women pingponging from an "Institute" to an "Academy," from massages to needles, from the acidic to the unctuous, from worry to despair.

Thank God, they regain their courage later on. Since I started my spa for applying makeup to my peers, I've never known a woman of fifty who was discouraged, or a sexagenarian who was neurasthenic. It's among these champions that it works to attempt—and to accomplish—makeup miracles. Where are the reds of yesteryear with their black-currant harshness, those unflattering whites, those babe-of-Mary blues? We have palettes that would make a painter drunk. The art of preparing faces, the makeup industry, excites almost as many millions as the movies. The harder an age is on women, the more women in their pride insist on hiding that they suffer from it. Crushing occupations take away her brief rest, even before daybreak, and we used to call her a "frail thing"! Heroically disguised in her tangerine makeup, her eyes enlarged, a small red mouth painted over her pale mouth, a woman retains, thanks to her daily lies, a daily dose of endurance, and the pride in never showing it.

I have never had as much respect for womankind, as much admiration as I had looking at her close up, as when I held reflected in a blue metallic light, her face without its secrets, rich in expression, varied under its agile wrinkles, or new and refreshed by having left behind for one moment its extraneous color. Oh, the struggle! But it's the struggle that keeps you young. I do my best, but you help me so much. When some of you whisper to me your true age, I'm dazzled. One woman throws herself into my little laboratory as if storming a barricade. She has an acid wit, down-to-earth, superb:

"Get to work, get to work!" she yells. "I've got a difficult sale. It's about looking thirty today, and I mean all day!"

From her brave optimism, sometimes I encounter, just long enough to part a curtain, one of those furtive young women who have a belly as thin as a greyhound, eyes reticent and velvety, who say little but who glance over the keyboard of makeup:

"This one . . . and this one. And then that thing for the eyes. And dark face powder. Oh! And then . . ."

I stop her. "And what more will you add when you're my age?"

One of them raises her glance and gives me a look stripped of illusions: "Nothing. If you think this is fun for me . . . My dream is to choose makeup so I don't have to do it again for the rest of my life. I wear a lot of makeup now so I can look the same in twenty years. That way I hope they don't see me change."

One of my great pleasures is discovery. One would not believe that so many feminine faces in Paris remain, to a ripe age, the way God created them. But when the dangerous hour comes, a sort of panic sets in, a desire not just to endure, but to be born. It's the season of the bitter, late spring of the heart, with its power to move mountains.

"Do you think it might be possible . . . Of course I know you can't turn me into a young woman. But I'd still like to try."

I listen, but above all I look. A large brown eyelid; an eye unaware of itself; a Roman cheek, a bit wide, but still firm; all this beautiful terrain to prospect, to brighten. Envy me. I get beautiful rewards from applying makeup: the sigh of hope; the astonishment, the arrogance that suddenly dawns; and that impatient glance toward the street, eager to see "what effect it will have," toward risk.

While I'm writing this, my daughter is still here. As she's reading, her hand drifts from a basket of fruit to a box of candy. She's a child of today. The gold of her hair—am I completely responsible for it? She had a peach complexion before becoming, despite winter, a dark nectarine, under a powder as reddish as the pollen of a spruce tree flower. She senses my eyes on her, shoots me a mischievous glance, and raises toward the light a bunch of grapes, black under a filmy layer of blue mist:

"Look," she says, "they're also wearing powder."

The Dancer's Song

When she worked in music halls, Colette danced as well as acted, though dance is also a metaphor in this piece. She first published this in a later edition of *Les Vrilles de la vigne* in 1934.

You call me a dancer, but I want you to know today that I never actually learned to dance. When you met me I was little and playful, dancing on roads and chasing my blue shadow. I spun like a bee, and a pollen of blond dust the color of a dusty path powdered my feet and my hair.

You saw me coming back from the fountain, cradling an amphora on the curve of my hip while the water, following the rhythm of my feet, leaped onto my tunic in round tears; in silver serpents; in short, curly spindles that rose, icy cold, up to my cheeks. I walked with a slow, serious gait, but you called my step a dance. You didn't look at my face, but you followed the motion of my knees, the sway of my waist, you read in the sand the shape of my naked heels, the imprint of my spread toes, which you compared to five pearls, each a different size.

You said to me, "Go gather flowers, chase that butterfly," because you called it a dance when I ran, whenever my body bowed to glance at a purple sweet William, and when I made the gesture, repeated at every flower, of throwing over my shoulder a slippery scarf.

At your house, alone with you and the turned-up wick of a lamp, you said to me, "Dance!" and I didn't dance.

But naked in your arms, tied to your bed with the smoldering ribbon of pleasure, you still called me a dancer, seeing desire leap under my skin, from my arched torso to my curved feet, that inevitable voluptuousness.

Weary, I put my hair up again, and you saw how docile it was, coiling around my forehead like a snake charmed by a flute.

I left your house while you murmured, "Your most beautiful dance isn't when you come running up to me, out of breath, full of angry desire, already tormenting the clasps of your dress as you run; it's when you withdraw from me, quiet, your knees bending, and as you withdraw you look at me, your chin perched on your shoulder. Your body remembers me, wavers, hesitates, your thighs miss me and your breasts thank me. You look at me, your head turned to the side, while your divining rod feet feel their way and choose their path.

"You leave, getting smaller and smaller, rouged by the setting sun, to the point where you're nothing more—when you reach the top of the slope, so skinny in your dress gone orange—than an upright flame, dancing imperceptibly."

If you don't leave me, I'll leave, dancing toward my white gravestone.

With an involuntary dance, each day a bit slower, I'll salute the light that made me beautiful and saw me loved.

In one last tragic dance I'll wrestle death, but I'll only struggle in order to surrender with grace.

May the gods grant me a harmonious fall, my arms crossed over my forehead, one leg folded, the other extended, as if to jump, with a light leap, over the black threshold of the kingdom of shadows.

You call me a dancer, but I still don't know how to dance.

Loves

Among her many gifts as a writer is Colette's remarkable ability to observe and record the behavior of animals. The cat described here is, according to the editors of the first volume of Colette's *Œuvres*, the cat whom Colette called *The Last Cat*, who is also the model for the cat in her novel called *The Cat*. Claude Farrère (1876–1957) was a prolific French novelist and a friend of Colette's. Paul Morand (1888–1976) was a French writer who authored plays, novels, and poetry. First published in a later edition of *Les Vrilles de la vigne* in 1934.

The robin redbreast won. Invisible, he entered the most dense area of the chestnut tree to sing about his victory in little dry cries. Face-to-face with the cat, he had not retreated. He had remained suspended in midair, a bit above her, vibrating like a bee, while he had tossed at her, in brief bursts, a discourse intelligible to whoever knows the haughty manner of a redbreast, and its bravura: "Tremble, you little fool! I am the redbreast! Yes, the redbreast in person! Take one more step, make just one little gesture in the direction of the nest where my mate is sitting on our eggs, and so help me, I'll tear your eyes out with this beak!"

I watched, ready to intervene, but the cat knows that redbreasts are sacred. She also knows that if she tolerates a bird's attack, she risks being ridiculed—she knows so many things. She beat her tail like a lion, her back quivered, but she yielded to the frenetic little bird, and the two of us are now resuming our twilight walk. A slow walk, pleasant, fruitful: the cat is making discoveries, and I'm educating myself. To put it more precisely, she *seems* to be making discoveries. She fixes on a point in the void, stops dead before something invisible, is startled by a noise I can't perceive. Then it's my turn, and I try to invent what is capturing her attention.

There's no risk in spending time with a cat, other than the risk that your life may become richer. I don't know whether it's on purpose that I've sought out the company of felines for the last half-century. I never have to look far: they appear right at my feet. A lost cat; a farm cat that hunts and is hunted, skinny with insomnia; a bookstore cat embalmed in ink; cats of cheese stores and butcher shops, well-fed but chilly, soles squarely on the tiles; wheezy cats of shopkeepers, bloated with scraps of lung meat; happy, despotic cats who reign over Claude Farrère, over Paul Morand—and over me. All of you meet me as if you're not surprised, and not displeased. Among one hundred cats, she testifies, one day, in my favor, this wandering and famished cat who threw herself, yelping, against the crowd disgorged by the Auteuil Metro station. She unraveled me from the others, recognized me: "Finally! What took you so long? I was at the end of my rope. Where's your home? Go ahead, I'm right behind you." She followed me, so sure of me that my heart beat hard. At first my home frightened her, because I wasn't alone. But she got used to it and stayed four years there, till her accidental death.

It would not be like me to forget you, warmhearted dogs, easily wounded, bandaged by nothing at all. How could I manage without you? You can't live without me. You make me feel I'm worth the price. Is there still a being for whom I replace everything? That's extraordinary, comforting—and a bit too easy. But let's hide that being with the eloquent eyes, let's hide him, as soon as he suffers his seasonal loves and a painful coupling rivets the female to the male. Quick, a folding screen, a tarpaulin, a beach umbrella—and after that, let's get going. And let's not come back for a whole week, at the end of which "He" won't even recognize "Her": "man's best friend" is rarely a dog's best friend.

I know more about the attachment he feels for me and about the exaltation he gets from it, than about the love life of dogs. It just so happens that I prefer, among the ten breeds I respect, those for whom the risks of maternity are forbidden. It happens that the Belgian terrier, the French bulldog—pug-nosed breeds with voluminous craniums, who often die while giving birth, instinctively forego the voluptuous semiannual benefits. Two of my female bulldogs bit males, and only accepted them as playmates during their innocence. A poodle, too discerning, refusing all suitors, found consolation in her voluntary sterility by pretending to nurse a red rubber puppy. Yes, there have been many dogs in my life—but there's also been the cat. To the species of cat I am indebted, to a certain degree, honorably, for the ability to deceive, for my enormous self-control, for an absolute aversion to harsh sounds, and for a need to remain silent for long periods.

This cat, who just posed for a tight close-up in the novel that bears her name, the cat with the robin-redbreast, I only celebrate her hesitantly and uneasily. Although she inspires me, she is obsessed with me. Without wanting to, I pulled her out of the feline world. She returns to it during mating season, but the handsome Paris tomcat, the stud who "comes to town" armed with his cushion, his litter box, his choice of meals, and . . . his grooming, what does my female do with him? The same thing she does with the stray cat with the cropped ears who comes through the gap in the hedge in the countryside. She makes quick use of him, furious and full of contempt. Chance couples this indifferent female with males she has never met. Loud cries reach me, of love and war, piercing cries like that of the great horned owl who announces the dawn. I recognize the voice of my cat in them, her insults, her snarls that set him straight and humiliate the victor who won her by chance.

In the country, she recovers some of her flirtatiousness. She becomes easy again, playful, unfaithful to several males she gives herself to and withdraws from without any scruples. It makes me happy to see that she can still be, at times, only "a cat," and not "the cat," that warm, lively, and poetic spirit, absorbed in the faithful love that she pledged to me.

Between the walls of a narrow garden in Île-de-France, she frolics, she lets herself go. She also resists. Intelligence has exempted her body from the common frenzy. She remains ice while her peers burn. But three weeks ago she dreamily calls to her lover under nests that are already empty, among kittens born two months earlier, and mixes her cries with those of the gray tit-bird chicks. Love does not need to be told twice. Comes the old striped conqueror, with enormous canines, dry, bald in spots, endowed with experience, with unparalleled decisiveness, and even the respect of his rivals. The young striped cat follows him closely, resplendent with self-confidence and foolishness, with a wide nose, a low forehead, and handsome as a tiger. On the tiles atop the wall, lastly the farm cat appears, his head dressed in two bands of gray against a dirty white background, not quite awake, and skeptical: "Was I dreaming or did I hear an urgent call?"

The three of them enter the lists, and I can say that they've seen some tough ones. First the female cat has a hundred hands to slap them, a hundred little hands, blue, rapid, clinging to their short fleece and to the skin they cover. Then she rolls herself into a figure eight. Then she sits down in the midst of the three tomcats and seems to forget about them for quite a while. Then she awakens from her lofty dream to perch on a crumbling pillar, where her virtue defies all attackers. When she condescends to descend, she stares at the three slaves with childish astonishment, deigns to allow one of them, with its muzzle, to kiss her dazzling and blue muzzle. The kiss goes on, she breaks it off with an imperious scream, a sort of cat's barking, untranslatable, but which the three males respond to by jumping back. In response, the female cat meticulously sets about her toilette, and the three deferred ones protest having to wait. They even pretend to fight one another, to pass the time, around a cold and deaf female cat.

Finally she gives up these lies and games, she makes herself welcoming, stretches to her full length, and, with a goddess's footstep, rejoins the world of mortals.

I didn't stay to see the next act. Since feline grace escapes undamaged from all dangers, why submit it to the supreme test? I abandoned the female cat to her demons and went back to meet her in the place that she leaves neither by day nor by night while I work slowly and painstakingly—the table where, unceasing, miraculously mute, but resonating with a muffled murmur of happiness, there lies, watches, or rests under my lamp, the cat, my model; the cat, my friend.

The Mirror

Claudine is the mischievous heroine of Colette's first four novels, including *Clau-dine at School*, bestsellers that the author set in a small town like the one where she grew up, in Burgundy. Since the novels were loosely based on Colette's early years, readers often confused the novelist with her main character. Renaud was Claudine's boyfriend, whom she marries. Willy (real name: Henri Gauthier-Villars) was Colette's first husband. Eugène Manuel (1823–1901) was a French playwright and poet. First published in the magazine *La Vie parisienne* in 1908, then in her book *Les Vrilles de la vigne* later that same year. Colette deleted this text from the last edition of this book that appeared in her lifetime, in 1950.

Frequently I run into Claudine. Where? You won't ever know. In the dim light of dusk, under the crushing sadness of a white and heavy noon, on nights that are moonless but clear, where you can just make out the glow of a naked hand raised to point out a star, I run into Claudine.

Today it's in the half-light of a darkened room, covered with a nondescript olive fabric, when the end of the day turns the color of an aquarium.

Claudine smiles and says, "Well, look who's here! If it isn't my double."

But I shake my head and answer, "I'm not your double. Haven't you had it up to here with that misunderstanding that binds us together, where we each reflect one another, where we each *mask* one another? You're Claudine, I'm Colette. Our faces, twins, have played hide-and-seek long enough. They loaned me Rézi, your blond friend, they married you off to Willy, when you were secretly pining for Renaud. Aren't you sick of it by now?"

Claudine hesitates, shrugs her shoulders, and answers vague-ly, "Who cares?" She sticks her right elbow into a cushion, and as if I'm imitating her, I prop up my left elbow with the same sort of cushion, and I find myself once more mirrored in a thick and cloudy crystal, since night is falling and the smoke from an abandoned cigarette spirals between us.

"Who cares?" she repeats.

But I know she's lying. Deep down, she's annoyed that she let me speak first. She cherishes me with a slightly vindictive tender-ness, which doesn't exclude a dignity that's just a drop bourgeois. To the fools who confuse us in good faith and compliment her on her talents as a mime, she responds stiffly, "That's not me who does pantomime. It's Colette." Vaudeville is not Claudine's cup of tea.

Faced with her stubborn indifference, I keep silent. I'm silent just today; but I'll go another round! I'm not done with this fight. I'll stand up to this double who looks at me with a face veiled by the dusk. Oh, my proud double! I won't dress in your clothes anymore. You can have it, that pure renunciation that says: after Renaud, no more feelings! You can have that noble shamelessness about confessing all your desires; that wifely charity—only in literature—that makes you tolerate all of Renaud's many flirtations. It's all yours, not mine, that fortress of loneliness where you slowly eat yourself up. That's where you discovered, at the zenith of your soul, a refuge that no invader can threaten. Stay there, ironic and sweet, and leave me my portion of uncertainty, love, unfruitful activity, delectable laziness, leave me my poor little human portion, which has its price.

Claudine, you've written the story of a part of your life, with a crafty candor that fascinated, for a while, both your friends and your enemies. From the slick and fertile cobblestones of Paris, to the depths of the sleepy and sweet-smelling provinces, thousands and thousands of Claudines are springing up, like she-devils who resemble us both. Plump and peevish girl-women; short-skirted; liberated, by a snip of the scissors, from their ribboned plaits of hair, or from their glossy buns, they'll lay siege to our husbands—intoxicated, giddy, dazzled. You didn't foresee, Claudine, that your gains would create that loss. No, I can't hold it against you, but still . . .

"Haven't you ever really, really wanted," I continue forcefully, "to wear a floor-length dress and have your hair pulled back flat, parted down the middle?"

Claudine's cheeks dimple into a smile. She follows my train of thought.

"Yeah," she admits. "But just to tease by being contrary. And what's that you've been saying about imitating? I admire how unaware you are, Colette. You cut your long hair short in imitation of me, remember?"

I hold up my hands to the heavens. "Lord, has it come to this! You're quibbling with me over foolishness like this? This is *mine*, this is *yours*. It's like we're acting parts in *The Dress*—oh, my childhood. *The Dress*, by the much-missed Eugène Manuel."

"Yes, our childhood . . ." sighs Claudine.

I knew she would say that. Claudine never misses a chance to bring up the past. All it takes are the words: "Do you remember . . ." and she relaxes, spills her secrets, completely surrenders. All it takes are the words: "Do you remember . . ." and she cocks her head at an angle with her watchful eyes, her ear straining toward the murmur of an invisible fountain. She turns on the charm again:

"When we were young . . ." she begins.

I nip that one in the bud. "Speak for yourself, Claudine. I've never been young."

She draws nearer with a little push of her stomach on the sofa, the kind of animal brusqueness that makes you fear getting bitten or pierced by a horn. She interrogates me, threatens me with her triangular chin:

"What? Are you trying to tell me that you were never young?"

"Never. I got older, but I was never young. I never changed. I remember myself with perfect clarity, with perfect melancholy. The same dark and demure heart, the same passionate taste for everything that breathes in an atmosphere of freedom, far from mankind—tree, flower, animals fearful and gentle, secret waters of useless streams—the same seriousness that quickly switches to exaltation without any cause. All of that is me as a child, and me right now. But what I've lost, Claudine, is my beautiful pride, the secret certainty of being that precious child, of feeling within me the extraordinary soul of an intelligent man, of a woman in love, a soul that can make my little body burst. Unfortunately, Claudine, I've lost almost all of that, in the process of becoming . . . only a woman. You remember the magnificent words our friend Calliope said to the man who was begging for her: "What great thing have you done that I should belong to you?" Those words, I wouldn't even dare to think them now, but I would have said them when I was twelve years old. Yes, I would've said them. You can't imagine what a queen of the earth I was at twelve! Firm, with a rugged voice, two tresses too tightly bound that whistled like the flick of a whip: leathery hands, scratched, crisscrossed with scars; a boy's square forehead that I now hide down to my eyebrows. Oh, you would've loved me when I was twelve years old—I miss myself so much!"

My double smiles, a joyless smile, that hollows out her dry cheeks, her cat-like cheeks that hold so little flesh between her wide temples and her narrow jaws.

"That's all you miss?" she says. "Then I envy you more than any other woman."

I remain silent, and Claudine doesn't seem to be waiting for my reply. Once more, I feel that the thinking of my double has joined itself to my own thinking, that they commingle passionately, silently. Joined, sprouting wings, giddy, they rise like the two velvety owls of this dusk turning greenish. Until what hour will they stay suspended in flight without coming asunder, above these two motionless and similar bodies, while night slowly devours their faces?

Gone Fishin'

This story takes place along the beaches of France that border the English Channel, with its extreme tides. The character of The Silent One is probably based on Colette's friend and confidant, Léon Hamel. The character of Maggie may be modeled after the writer Meg Villars, who married Colette's first husband after Colette divorced him. First published in *Les Vrilles de la vigne*, 1908.

FRIDAY.—Marthe says, "Kids, we're going fishing tomorrow at the Headlands! Café au lait for everyone at eight. Anyone who's not ready, the car leaves behind." And I lowered my head and said, "Terrific!" with a submissive joy, and not without irony. Marthe, a combative creature, inflicts happiness in a harsh tone of voice and with abrupt gestures. Decisively she lays out the agenda for our holiday: "We'll have lunch there, on the beach. We'll take you, and then The Silent One, who'll carry all the fish, and also Maggie, so she can finally wear her pretty new bathing outfit."

With that, she turned on her heels. From afar I see, on the terrace that commands the sea, her reddish-brown bun of hair, questioning the horizon with a threatening and challenging glance. I think I can tell from the way she's shaking her little warrior's brow that she's muttering, "Just you let it rain tomorrow, and you'll see." She comes back inside, and rescued from the pressure of her stare, the sun can set in peace beyond the Bay of Somme, a humid and flat desert where the sea, as it pulls back, has left oblong lakes, round pools, vermillion canals where horizontal rays are bathing. The dunes are mauve, with a rare head of hair made of bluish grass, an oasis of delicate convolvulus, their pink-veined umbrella skirts torn by the wind when they open.

The thistles on the dunes, in azured sheet metal, mixing with the rest harrow flowering carmine, rest harrow that pricks with a thorn so short that you don't suspect it. Meager and hardy flora, that hardly ever wilt, and brave the wind and the salty waves, flora that match our combative little hostess, that handsome reddish thistle, with the look of a shameless schoolboy.

Yet here and there the sea fennel turns green, fat, juicy, acidulous, the lively and tender flesh of dunes pale as snow. When Marthe, my annoying friend, exasperates everyone, when you're ready—because of her look of a young fury, her boyish voice—to forget that she's a woman, then Marthe laughs abruptly, adjusts a reddish lock of hair that came loose, showing her arms, light-colored, glowing, which you want to bite and which would crunch, cool, acidulous, and juicy to the tooth like sea fennel.

The Bay of Somme, still humid, darkly reflects an Egyptian sky, raspberry, turquoise, and ash green. The sea has retreated so far out that you have to wonder if it will ever come back. Yes, it will return, treacherous and furtive as I know it here. You don't think of it; you read on the sand, you play, you sleep, facing the sky—right until a cold tongue insinuates itself between your big toes and rips from you a nervous yell: the sea is there, just flat, it has covered twenty kilometers of beach with the silent speed of a snake. Before we could anticipate, it has soaked a book, blackened a white skirt, drowned the croquet set and tennis racquets. Five minutes more, and there it is hitting the wall of the terrace, with a soft and rapid slap-slapping, with the submissive and content motion of a dog wagging its tail.

A dark bird zooms out from the sunset, an arrow shot by the dying sun. It passes over my head with the rustling of stretched silk, and it changes, against the darkening west, into a snowy seagull.

SATURDAY MORNING, 8:00 a.m.—Blue and gold fog, cool wind, all is well. Marthe is delivering an oration below and the multitudes tremble, prostrate. I'm rushing: will I arrive in time to keep her from putting too much pepper on the potato salad?

8:30 a.m.—We leave! The car purrs, decorated with floating shrimp nets. From deep within a greenish raincoat, from behind a pair of convex lenses, Marthe's voice vituperates against the clumsy zeal of the maids: "Those blockheads stuck the apricots right against the cold roast pork!" Still, she condescends to offer me a gloved paw, and I surmise that she's smiling at me with a deep-sea diver's grace. Maggie, barely awake, slowly becomes conscious of the outside world and smiles in English. We know all that she's hiding under her long overcoat, a bathing outfit right out of a vaudeville routine (the shrimp-fishing scene). The Silent One, who speaks not a word, smokes energetically.

8:45 a.m.—On the flat road that twists unnecessarily and hides, around each bend, a peasant and his cart, Marthe, at the wheel, brakes a bit suddenly and grumbles in her diving suit.

8:50 a.m.—Sharp turn, peasant and cart. Lurch to the left. Marthe yells, "Cuckold!"

9:00 a.m.—Sharp turn: in the middle of the road, a little boy and his wheelbarrow full of manure. Lurch to the right. Marthe just brushes the kid and yells, "Cuckold!" Already? Poor kid.

9:20 a.m.—The sea, to the left, between the rounded dunes. And that sea is even farther out than it was yesterday evening. My companions assure me that while I was dozing it rose right up to that fringe of pink shells, but I don't believe it for a minute.

9:30 a.m.—The Shacks! Three or four black coffins, made of tarred planks, stain the dune, the dune of a sand so pure here, so delicately mamillated by the wind, that it makes you think of snow, of Norway, of lands where winter never ends.

> *Without moving, yet rolled,*
> *The fine sand hollows out an alcove*
> *Where, despite the cries of the mauve*
> *Seagull, one can hide, and the dune molds*
> *A bed in its charming folds*

murmurs The Silent One, a modest poet. Marthe, excited, leans over the wheel and . . . sinks two of the car's tires. Faster than a little bulldog, she jumps out, gauges the damage, and calmly declares: "This spot is good, anyway. Farther up the road I couldn't turn."

We arrive at the end of the earth. The dune, completely naked, shelters between its rounded knees the black shacks, and in front of us lies the desert that deceives and fortifies, the desert under a white sun, its gilding washed out by the mist of hot days.

10:00 a.m.: "Papuan Tribe Conjuring the Spirit of the Bitter Waters"—that's the caption I'll write on the back of the snapshot that Maggie just took. The "natives," with heads like wet seals, in the water up to their waists, strike the sea with long poles, howling rhythmically. They beat the fish into a net stretched across an elongated lake, a huge arm of the sea abandoned here by the tide's neglect. Brill are swarming there, and bay shrimp, and flounder, and sand dabs. Marthe flings herself out and digs around the moving sand banks, like a good ratter. I imitate her, first taking tentative steps, because all my skin bristles to feel passing between my ankles something flat, alive, and shiny.

"Get it, get it! Good God! Can't you see it?"

"What?"

"A sand dab, a sand dab, right there!"

There? Yes, a flat plate, covered in mother-of-pearl, that flashes and escapes between two waves. Heroically I search the sea bottom, down on all fours, flat on my belly, dragging along on my knees. A quick yelp: Marthe cries out in triumph and her streaming arm raises the flat plate that writhes and lashes. I'll die of jealousy if I come back empty-handed. Where is The Silent One? The coward, he's fishing with a shrimp net. And Maggie? She's fine, she's swimming, only worried about her figure and her suit of raspberry silk. I'm only competing against Marthe, Marthe and her cap of red hair stuck to her head, Marthe knotted up in a huge blue jersey, a little sailor with a round behind. The critters, the critters, I can sense them, they're mocking me. A large sand eel in mother-of-pearl flashes from the soft sand, draws in the air a sparkling monogram with its serpent's tail, and dives back down.

11:00 a.m.—The Papuan tribe has finished its conjuring. The Spirit of the Bitter Waters, responsive to ritual howling, has filled their nets to the brim with flat fish. On the sand, still held captive in the tarred mesh, the beautiful, suffering plaice, with their very moving bellies; the insipid flounder; the brill indelibly spattered with blood. But I only want the prey hunted down by my own flayed hands, between my knees scraped by sand and sharp shells. The brill, I know it now, it's a big canary that nosedives between my ankles drawn together and gets jammed there—the sand dab is just as dumb. We fish side by side, Marthe and I, and the same yelp escapes from both of us when the catch is good.

11:30 a.m.—The sun bakes our napes, our shoulders emerging from the warm and caustic water. The waves, under our tired gazes, dance in blue-green moiré patterns, in gold rings, in broken necklaces. Ouch, my back! I look for my mute companions: The Silent One arrives, just like Marthe, completely beat, groans, "I'm hungry!" The Silent One smokes, and his huge cigar only leaves him enough room for a proud smile. He holds out to us his shrimp net overflowing with live mother-of-pearl.

Now it's Maggie's turn to come back, delighted with herself. She caught seven shrimp and a baby sole.

"Time for soup, kids!" yells Marthe. The natives transport the catch to the car.

"Are we taking it all? There's at least fifty pounds!"

"First of all, it boils down a lot when you cook it. We'll eat some fried tonight, tomorrow morning with grated cheese on top, tomorrow night in a court bouillon. So we'll cook some ourselves, and maybe give some to the neighbors."

1:00 p.m.—Seated in a tent, we eat lunch, gradually sobering up. Down there, at the bottom of the blinding and shadowless desert, something is boiling mysteriously, purrs, and comes closer—the sea! Champagne doesn't galvanize us, a headache hovers over our hardworking heads.

We contemplate one another without generosity. Marthe has gotten sunburnt on her little bulldog nose. The Silent One yawns and chews his fifth cigar. Maggie shocks us a bit, too white and too naked, in her raspberry suit.

"What is that smell?" Marthe shouts. "It stinks of musk, and I don't know what else."

"It's the fish. The nets are hanging over there, full."

"My hands stink, too. It's the flounder that smells musky and rotten. What if we give a little bit of fish to the nice natives?"

2:00 p.m.—Mournful trip home. We're secretly sniffing our hands. Everything smells like raw fish: the cigar of The Silent One, Maggie's suit, Marthe's moist hair. The west wind, soft and burning, smells like fish. The car exhaust, and the dune glazed with blue shadows, and this whole day, it all smells of fish.

3:00 p.m.—Back home. The villa smells like fish. Fierce, nauseated, Marthe shuts herself in her room. The cook knocks on her door:

"Would Madame tell me if she wants the sand dabs fried or with grated cheese tonight?"

A door bursts open furiously and Marthe's voice vociferates:

"Do me a favor and make all that sea crap disappear from this house. And for the next week, I forbid you to serve anything but soft boiled eggs and roast chicken!"

Masked Ball on the Riviera: Cyclamen and Buttercup, or the Costume Ball of the Feet

This story shares the Belle Époque setting of Colette's *Gigi*, her most famous work of fiction. The costume ball Colette is describing has a color theme: yellow and mauve, a combination that doesn't sit well with the narrator. The party takes place in freewheeling Monte Carlo, where courtesans and theater people mix freely with aristocrats. The characters are real people, party animals of that era. Colette half-disguised their names by leaving out certain letters, but her readers would have guessed the identities of these tabloid celebrities. In the first volume of Colette's *Œuvres*, the editors identify several of the characters. Eve Lavallière and Suzanne Derval were two of the leading actresses in France at this time. Derval is said to be one of the models for the character Léa in Colette's novel *Chéri*. Emilienne d'Alençon was a well-known dancer and courtesan, called one of the "three Graces" of the demi-monde of turn-of-the-century France, along with Caroline Otero and Liane de Pougy (who also appear in this piece). Henry Bernstein was a French playwright. Princess P. is Princess Poniatowska, a member of the Polish royal family, and therefore a relative of the great Mexican writer and activist, Elena Poniatowska. Jean Lorrain was a writer and dandy of turn-of-the-century France, openly gay. This piece was first published in *Les Vrilles de la vigne* in 1908, but Colette deleted it from later editions of that book.

I hope no one feels slighted by this subtitle! I don't want to cause the inhabitants of Nice any offense, no matter how minor. But what do you expect? The only thing anyone talked about at this costume ball at the municipal casino is feet, feet, and more feet. "Oh, my feet!" "God, my feet are killing me!" "I can't even feel my feet anymore." "I can hardly stand on my feet."

From up on the balcony, I see swirling, glowing, swinging, trampling, a mauve and yellow nightmare, cyclamen and buttercup. Oh, the tiresome and insipid pairing of this too-pink mauve and this lifeless yellow! From here, the two shades blend, drink one another, blurred by dust. It looks (excuse the expression)—it looks a bit like vomit. My eye hunts in vain for a vigorous velvety violet, a solid and joyous orange, an old gold tinted green or lustrous bronze. Instead, instead, I swim, with a glance distracted and already overwhelmed, on a mauve and yellow swell, cyclamen, buttercup, cyclamen, buttercup. I need to drink some lemonade without sugar, or a sip of old cognac.

Examining this nauseating ensemble more closely, the costumes, at least, look clean: many achieve elegance, some have attempted an exaggerated sumptuousness. Under my anonymous smock of a lemon Pierrot, I wander heroically, jostled, stepped on—oh, my feet!—and I eventually recognize certain silhouettes: a way of holding one's head, a shade of blond, a young little devil happy to shout abuse from under his black velvet mask without fear of retribution. A little mauve clown bounces up to me and pulls me along, silently. With shining eyes under a black mask, moving too quickly for me to read, but with legs of fine, hard spindles, her precious ankles give her away as Eve Lav . . . ère. Another clown, better behaved, stops us, scolds us by shaking a finger, and smiles without saying a word; but he displays his attractive mouth, with bright teeth, and when he turns away, that wide nape, that white and rich neck, so stubborn, reveal that the clown is Suzanne De . . . val. Handsome and calm clown, you, too, sigh as you walk away, "Oh, my feet!"

Emilienne d'Al . . . has generously taken off her mask, over-come with heat and proud of her smart costume: "a Neapolitan fisherman," she informs us: short, tight pants held up by a gypsy-style belt with fringes, Spanish bolero hat, and a short Venetian coat thrown over her shoulders. "Oh, my feet!" sighs Mademoi-selle d'Al . . . , collapsing into a chair. "Kids, I can't stand it any-more, I think I'm going to take off my shoes!"

Tall, tall, tall, in his yellow domino mask, Henri B . . . st . . . n stalks the hallways, his nostrils flaring, his hands hungry for some-thing, terribly hungry for something.

A yellow domino mask in a cascade of mauve silk muslin, two dangerously blue eyes, and that flashing mouth. I've seen that mouth smiling in the opera ballet, haven't I, Mademoiselle Ric . . . i?

A violet frock, and under it almost masculine shoulders swing to and fro: a hood hides the forehead, sleeves cover the fingertips—but nothing could disguise that look, alternately care-less and cruel; that mouth, fine and pinched like an aging Caesar; that whole face, asexual and so spirit-of-evil: why, if it isn't Princess P.!

Everything's whirling, whirling: I'm going to be seasick if I keep staring at the mauve and yellow eddies. They unfurl, down below, against the officials in charge of the ball, sad little black islands, somber reefs that stagger but resist—I admire you, cham-pions of order and morality, breakwaters, sea walls! (If my name was just Willy, I'd even say, "sea walls, see waltz." But you can't have everything!)

Let's dance! And I take into my arms, as an eager Pierrot, a gracious mauve domino mask, a svelte, supple blond, who, unaware, steps on her train of satin and soft muslin, and we turn, we turn, carried along, squished, pushed, till we reach one of those little black islands standing against the storm. Surprise! The little island reacts, stops us with a polite but inflexible arm, and its rough policeman's voice says to us, "Separate, please, ladies. It's forbidden here for women to waltz together. Rules of decorum, you know [*sic*]."

Oh, Nice, oh carnival in Nice! You whom my friend Jean Lorrain painted with the most tempting vices, how they maligned you!

Around four in the morning, we end up at the Restaurant du Cercle, which I won't say anything about—other than that we consumed bouillon, fatty salmon, nondescript beef tournedos, leathery chicken, and ham, and that it cost twenty-five louis for eight people, without dessert, not including the tip.

Monte Carlo: A strange place, one that I hardly know, and one that scares me. Uneasiness. A chill down my spine, my head feels too hot. Nervous pacing, since I don't know where to rest, where to get tired. From Beausoleil to the sea, the city spills down to the Casino; irresistibly, you slide downhill to the Casino—after which there are only rocks, water.

Toward the end of the day, in the gaming rooms, all that anxious humanity, struggling, sweating, suffering, coveting, and despairing, smells almost like a stable. I'm a bit bored, since I hardly ever gamble. "You just don't know how to bet," the lucky Jeanne de B . . . lne insists in an authoritarian voice. "Just watch what I do." She tosses a gold louis on the number 26—and the ball just happens to land on that. Miracle of miracles! I keep quiet and I admire, but Countess R. shrugs her shoulders and sticks stubbornly to her system of inverses: she plays 13 after 31, 32 after 23. But what does she bet after 35? I don't dare ask her, since I don't know how to play. I prefer to watch. So many beautiful women! They bet, almost all of them, and passionately. When they've placed their bets a mysterious poison purples their cheeks, injects their eyes, and changes the shape of their noses.

Frail, delicious, supported, almost carried by the young H. and by G., just as young, Madame L. de P . . . y passes by. She has the lovely smile of a happy young mother leaning on her two strapping sons. Less frail, but not less beautiful, Madame C . . . Ot . . . o passes by, not gambling today, her forehead shrouded with a strange melancholy. "Alas," she answers her anxious admirers, "it's because tomorrow I begin my twenty-ninth year." The de la R. couple are much observed, especially the wife, that compulsive and wealthy gambler. Madame de la R., whose little dry hands sow and harvest fistfuls of gold and precious filthy paper. Her gloved hands, her bodice, her hat, her face drained of color—all are white. She resembles a pale bird with her aquiline beak, and her pale eyes cast a spell over the gold.

Let's leave this place. The moon is rising and my fever will be soothed by the treacherous wind at twilight, all along the dangerous and charming road that borders the sea as far as Nice. Already, under a full moon, a long reflection glows on the water, a silver spindle, pearly as the belly of a fish. We will go farther than Beaulieu, and Villefranche, where the fleet is sleeping, immobile and illuminated, sheltered in its narrow cove. And I'll smile, reassured, when the wheels of the car just slightly graze, as we arrive home, the orange trees of the park at Villa Cessole.

Springtime in Nice.—Gorgeous South of France, you please me, but I don't love you. You seduce me because you shine, because your irresistible sun warms my shoulders with a rough caress, makes me more active than a lizard running in circles on a heated rock, and plays on the sea that comes to life and turns pale just as it pleases. But I don't love you. You bloom, deceitful, eager, South of France, and your jonquil, your violet, your pale pink almond, don't wait for the true springtime—what do I care about flowers without leaves, without their tender leaves, rolled up into trumpets and pointed like little ears of fauns? The grass on your slopes turns green, but pricks and doesn't bleed, when I step on it, that pale and sugary blood with its intoxicating perfume.

Your eternal greenery, palm trees and cactus, aloes and wintering rose bushes, they wound my hand, tear my dress. In the end, you lying South of France, you bloom without fragrance. In vain, amidst the banal perfume of your flowers, my forest soul begs for the odor of the earth itself, the sovereign odor of the living soil, fertile, moist. The amorous gesture that makes me lean, nostrils wide open, toward a meadow watered by a warm rain, finds no reward here; you're only dry white powder and rock in bloom.

There is less spring among these roses, under these orange trees luminous with ripe oranges, than in one single day of thaw, back there, in my land with its veiled hills! Pretty, deceitful South of France, I would give all these roses, all the light, all the fruit, for a warm and fresh February afternoon, where, in the land I love, the bluish snow melts slowly in the shadow of hedges, and uncovers, bit by bit, the stiff young wheat, such a moving green. On the thorn bush, still black, a glossy thrush gurgles melodiously, releases its limpid and round notes—and the scent of the unbound earth, that aroma rises over carpets of dead leaves that have been steeping for four months, triturated by frost and rain, filling my heart with the bitter and incomparable happiness of spring.

Shipwrecked on a Traffic Island

The Madeleine is a church that looks on the outside like a Greek temple, located near the fashionable Place de la Concorde in Paris. In classical mythology, Princess Andromeda was chained to a rock to be devoured by a sea monster as a punishment for her mother's arrogance, but Perseus rescued Andromeda. First published in *Paris-Journal* on March 2, 1910.

"Oh, it's only you, Hamond? Come in. Don't peek. I'm wearing my putting-on-makeup hat. Have a seat. Not on the dog, you silly man!"

Hamond, a portrait painter, is one of my newest old friends; but certain emotional accidents have strengthened our affection for one another, and we now think of each other as childhood buddies, even though he's approaching fifty. Fifty autumns have gilded, tanned, thinned out his long face with his knightly nose, and if this ordinary man resembles Don Quixote, that's not his fault!

For three years we have played together the game of "telling our woes." As fate would have it, at the moment when my marriage was breaking up, the very young and lying Madame Hamond left the conjugal home, abandoning her husband right when he was in the middle of painting her portrait.

Poor Hamond! I saw this betrayed older lover shed tears; he witnessed and sympathized with my crises of silence that had turned to revolt, he recounted unpublished anecdotes about my ex; and I in turn recalled some words from his crazy young wife.

"Do you remember when. . . ."

For us, those were picnics of black melancholy, which left us exhausted, older, disgusted by it all . . . until the miraculous day when we discovered together, fearfully, that we were very happy to have lost—he, his wife; me, the cause of my suffering.

We didn't tell a soul.

To the whole world, he continued to be "that poor Hamond." Sometimes we would exchange a glance, like gleeful accomplices, when my friend came and knocked at the door of my dressing room at the music hall. He hardly paints anymore, he strolls, he's free, happy, on his own. His large nose inhales the delights of life. He disappears for weeks at a time and returns in a great mood, revealing his happiness only through deep sighs.

He and my dresser are the only ones allowed to enter my dressing room while I mould onto my face Vaseline, white face, rouge, while my scarf made into a hat turns me into a billiard ball or a doll without a wig, as it does this evening.

"It's only you, Hamond? Come in."

He sits down behind me, and his long silence ends up intriguing me. I turn around. "Lord, *what* is the matter with you, Hamond?"

He lifts his head with the expression of a sad collie, his eyes filled with a sorrow beyond remedy.

"What's the matter? My wife is the matter. I've taken her back."

"You've taken her back? Whatever for, you silly man!"

He scratches the rug with the end of his cane, as if he doesn't dare answer just yet.

"Because . . . Because last Saturday she was on the traffic island in the middle of the rue Royale, in front of the Madeleine."

Furiously I lift my shoulders. "But that's idiotic, Hamond! Is this some kind of a joke?"

"It's not a joke," he says slowly. "Look. You know how bad the traffic is in Paris around six in the evening."

"I know, I know. Get to the point!"

"No, I can't get to the point!" he cries bitterly. "Let me tell you the whole story, good God, if you want to know everything! The traffic, as I was saying, is very bad around six o'clock, particularly around the Madeleine. I was on my way there in a taxi, almost at the Madeleine, on the rue Royale. It's absolute chaos there. A sticky fog, cars bumping one another, pedestrians stuck on the sidewalk too long and getting angry, cursing the traffic cops, and then like crazy people, the pedestrians start to cut right into six lanes of traffic. In short, it was your everyday riot. My taxi purred patiently by the traffic island. The one with the clock, you know? Three or four madwomen who were squawking on the sidewalk started to cross right at the moment when the whole mass of cars began to move forward again, and one of the women, slightly bruised by the hood of a car, stepped onto the little traffic island and stood there petrified, right in the headlights of a limousine. It was my wife."

"So?"

"So, I saw her there, but she didn't see me for half a minute. She had on a stupid hat, the kind she always likes. But underneath it, what a face! Her mouth was open, she was out of breath with fear, holding her skirt with one hand, and with the other a shiny fur, and pressed against her she held a little purse, an umbrella, I don't even know what else, twitching with terror, with a look like Andromeda gave the monster—it broke my heart. She stood there, her back against the gas lamp, with the expression of a shipwrecked woman who stares, glued to a reef, while the seas are rising. I . . . I don't know what happened to me. Suddenly I yelled inwardly, 'You see her? You see that face of a drowning woman, that horrible look of an abandoned animal who doesn't know where to turn for help? It's your fault that she's there, weak, hunted, miserable, sinful. You can take her back, lift her with one gesture to your island, save her. Do it, do it!' "

"And did you?"

"I did," admits my old friend, sadly. "I threw open the door of the taxi, I pulled that shipwrecked woman to me. She's at my house now. She has no idea what happened. She thinks I still love her, and that *she* took *me* back. So, she's taking advantage of the situation, she makes decisions, parades around, recites her speeches all over the house, in *my* house! And so here I am again, very . . . very unhappy."

Colette's Advice Column

Colette had an advice column in the women's magazine *Marie Claire* during the years 1939 and 1940. The first letter-writer refers to Saint Catherine's Day, November 25. Saint Catherine is the patron saint of unmarried women. In France, during this period, friends would be supportive of single women on that day and sometimes organize a party where a woman could meet a prospective husband.

From Denise in Despair:

In May, I met a young man. At the beginning he told me he loved me, and since I had never flirted, never known another young man, I put all my trust in him. I still love him with all my soul. From the start, he didn't hide from me that he had flirted before, but he swore to me that he would love only me from then on. So we saw each other for a month and a half, and at the end of June he left town for a three-month vacation, and went home to stay with his parents in N. During those three months, he didn't write to me. When he returned in October for his third year of teacher training college, we reconnected and clearly enjoyed being together again. A week after this meeting, he wrote to me a letter full of remorse, doubts, telling me that he wasn't worthy of my love (since I'd never stopped loving him and thinking of him despite his silence). In this letter, he asks my forgiveness for having made me suffer and promises to try to change in order to be worthy of a love as pure as mine, as he says. Then he tells me that he never liked me as in "love," he just wanted to flirt; he realizes that he was wrong. He says he feels for me a very, very strong friendship. He still writes to me and keeps asking my forgiveness and says he wants to always be a sincere friend to me. In other words, there hasn't been a break-up at all. On Saint Catherine's Day, he sent me a card with these words: "Georgette, permit me to wish you a happy Saint Catherine's Day; I hope you welcome my card. Your sincere friend, Jean." His words are simple, but they touch me deeply. Tell me, dear Marie Claire, do you think love can grow from a great friendship? Answer me, please, I'm in such despair. It causes Jean a great deal of pain to see me in such despair. He says to me: "Don't get discouraged, my little Georgette. Don't make yourself sick over this. I'm not worthy of a deep love like yours."

You see, for him, I'm completely different from the girls he knew before, because I have a beautiful concept of love; for me, it's something sacred; you should only love one time, I believe, and

I really feel I'll never love another besides him. I love him exclusively, as my only love. He asks me to promise that I'll get over my pain, but I can't: I keep having these crises of crazy despair. I can never be consoled. Should I hope?

Besides, I'm very pretty, everyone says so. And I'm always getting compliments, but it disgusts me, I can tell you; I'd prefer to be ugly and to be loved by the one I love so much. Some girls tell me I'm really wrong to suffer for a guy, that I'm not modern, that I'd do better to have fun with whoever, but this negative advice disheartens me. I don't go out much; I'm going to be twenty years old and I have to do all the housework myself for my family. The people who know me admire my courage, I never complain, but it's hard, this life.

P.S. Right now, Jean has no relationships with other girls. I think he really wants to change, and be more serious.

Colette's Response:

He has "recognized his mistakes" and he signs his letter, "Your sincere friend, Jean." Can you doubt that it's all over between you?

If he liked you as someone to love, he might have signed his letter, "Your worst enemy who adores you, Jean." Then he wrote you, "I'm not worthy . . ." and he told you his "doubts." Leave all hope behind. If you were the one distant from him, and he still loved you, wouldn't you, in order to leave him, in order no longer to carry the burden—intolerable—of an unrequited love, wouldn't you forego this gesture (which lacks nobility) of making yourself ugly in someone else's eyes? But that's what Jean is doing. To begin with, he says he's "unworthy." Even worse, he talks about "friendship," a decoy, a scarecrow for young lovers, that he offers as a consolation. How would he know that between a man and a woman friendship is a temperate and delicious climate where love takes refuge when it has given up all its fruits and serenely welcomes old age? Jean speaks about humility. Why not also the respect that he has for you? Such great virtues in him seem like a fake beard; they are insignificant next to his charming faults, often just an ornament for his prerogative of being twenty years old, thoughtless, spontaneous, demanding, jealous. How moving your postscript is! "Jean wants to change, become serious, he doesn't see other girls." All the more reason to give this way-too-clever

Jean the time to develop his character far away from you, and hope that he will see, on the contrary, other girls. Pretty, serious, hardworking—do you fear the comparisons?

In a few months, I hope you will laugh about ever having written the words, "crazy despair . . . never, never . . . my only love."

Wait. Remain, in your own eyes and in the eyes of others, the way you are. Refuse to "have fun with whoever." It's not a pretty thing, a young woman without restraints. Besides, I'm not worried about you. You're not among those for whom pleasure can substitute for happiness.

From A Tormented Heart:

I hope you can enlighten me and restore to my soul my peace of mind and my joy in life. I'm twenty years old, I've been engaged now for six months to a man who is twenty-seven and who, I can assure you, adores me. Before meeting him, I went out several times with another young man whom I liked a lot, but then, when I left the city where he lives, I forgot about him a little bit. Now I'm back, but tied to my fiancé. I've seen that young man again and my love has rekindled. I feel I love him more than my fiancé, or rather, not in the same way: I feel for him a violent love, passionate, reckless; for my fiancé, my love is calm, considered, as if asleep. I agreed to go out with him again, confessing to him I was engaged. He tells me he loves me but I know I can't have any hope for a future with him. But my reason does me no good, my love is stronger than my reason. I'm abandoning my fiancé little by little, I suffer from the thought that he will suffer if he finds out about this and still I'm leaning more and more to the other man. I can't see clearly anymore, I'm all nerves, help me, will you? I'm confident that your response can bring me peace.

Colette's Response:

On the one hand, you love; on the other, you're loved. In the first place, you want to keep what's lavished on you; in the second, you want to give all.

Tormented Heart, I'm not going to suggest bigamy to you. Besides, what is it that really torments you? When you're twenty years old, do you listen to a love that is "calm, pondered, as if asleep"? Your age is not made for well-motivated decisions, and it seems to me you are looking more for excuses than advice. You admit that absence was enough to make you forget "a little bit" the man who, once you found him again, set you on fire. Couldn't you try, using such efficient means, to forget him "a lot"? And at the same time—honesty invites you—find the courage not to marry the fiancé who only inspires in you lukewarm feelings. As far as I can see, he is lacking in insight and shrewdness. How can he not sense around you, around him, a presence, and thoughts, that are against him? Leave him be, the angel; and leave the tempter.

Does my response not bring you the "peace" you crave? Excuse my frankness, but I can't help remembering that you are twenty years old. And I've never been able to believe that peace is a good present to give a young woman.

From Minerva:

Colette calls this letter-writer Minerva, after the Roman goddess of wisdom.

Marie Claire, my case will probably seem very simple to you. I'm just terribly indecisive. Here's what it's all about:

I'm twenty-six years old and I've been married for two and a half years. My husband and I make a good couple; we adore one another; he never goes out without me and vice versa.

I have a very good job, not very well paid for the moment (a thousand francs a month), but the pay promises to go up over the years. My husband earns a bit more than I do; our combined income allows us to live simply; we sometimes have to do without some pleasure, some personal item, but we're happy.

I have to tell you that we owe a fairly large amount that we are paying off slowly but surely. It's going to continue like this for a few years.

I have the opportunity to have, in a city which is not the one where I live, a job that would pay me as much as my current one (which is only part-time); I could accept the second job and double my income and, in this way pay off our debt very quickly and live much more freely.

All this is very well, isn't it, Marie Claire, but I can see up the road; sometimes I will have to be away for two or three days at a time, or come home very late at night. Don't you think these frequent absences put my lovely household at risk? Won't my husband resume the habits he had as a young man? I know he doesn't want to cause me any pain, but should I resent it if he goes out with friends, if he goes to a café? He's just like a big kid!

I'm putting my case before you, Marie Claire, and I will follow your advice blindly. My happiness might depend on the decision I make. I haven't spoken to my husband about this job, because then I have to reveal my fears to him and I don't want him to have doubts about it himself. Do you understand?

Thank you, Marie Claire.

Colette's Response:

It evokes great sympathy, madame, your letter to Marie Claire. What sound judgment, what thirst to confront all your responsibilities, what reasonable impatience to strengthen and enlarge your work situation! A letter written in good French by a good Frenchwoman. You've imagined what could happen with good luck and bad. Strong enough to take on new responsibilities, you tremble only for love and its sweet routine. I would like to relieve you of that faint-heartedness.

Love, which often sustains itself on almost nothing, a hope, a plan, a minute of presence, fears certain superabundances, and especially familiarity. Its motto is the same as yours: "Always together!" up until the moment when the happy couple secretly thinks: "What? Together again?" All that one-on-one can be terribly asphyxiating. Let me scare you a little by telling you about a husband, suffocated by his routine happiness, who hid from his wife in order to taste a strawberry ice cream; or to breathe on his own in the park, under the acacias in bloom, alone, completely alone, voluptuously alone.

I'm delivering the memory of this escapee to your lucid mind, madame. You accept fairly serenely, it seems to me, the idea of the brief separations, when profitable, that the future holds for you. Yes, I know exactly what you mean, you trust yourself, but that "big kid . . ." Do that big kid the honor of trusting him and treating him like an honest man: take the second job you've been offered, its material advantages, the weight of the work—and its risks. You are at an age to take smart risks. It's not bad that a decision that's a bit adventurous, generating tender worries, has shaken up your current wisdom. With all my heart I wish you, young Minerva, the good luck you well deserve.

"I love a young man . . ."

In her response to this letter Colette refers to a nineteenth-century romance novel, Octave Feuillet's *The Novel of a Poor Young Man.*

Dear Marie Claire:

I love a young man—every day moves him farther away from me. I have loved him for six months and I suffer with my whole soul. He guesses my feelings. I'm beautiful and rich. I think he loves me a little, but I had the impression that he would never declare that love.

He is fleeing me now, avoids me as much as possible. I feel discouraged and detach myself little by little from life, so great is my sadness. My father owns an important agricultural business that he runs himself. This young man is a simple foreman, like many of my father's employees. His distinguished manner, his culture, his education, and his handsome physique really intrigued me when I first saw him in these reduced circumstances. Then his serious and calm manner got me interested in him. His eyes, above all, reflect something indefinable, but I think it's a deep sadness. What terrible suffering he must have endured! When we exchange glances, his sometimes shakes me to the point where I can't suppress a nervous trembling. Now I love him deeply, with all my soul.

I'm a woman of the world, I entertain many people, but never has a man made such an impression on me. I learned later from a certain person that he belongs to a rich farming family. Hardworking and energetic, he took charge at the age of twenty-two of a large enterprise belonging to his father that he ran himself, very competently. Then a financial disaster completely ruined his family. Now he is twenty-nine years old. I'm twenty-one.

My father, very authoritarian and strict in matters of suitability, will never accept a union that arises from such circumstances. What to do, Marie Claire? I wish I could be poor to live by His side and help him to suffer!

L.

Colette's Response:

What do to? Get married, mademoiselle, on the condition that, as I've said before, his heart responds to yours. The most pressing thing is to be happy. You are held back by a father who is "very authoritarian"? But this father knows very well that his authority, when it comes to a daughter who has reached the age of consent, does not go any farther than to deprive her of money—and yet! Your letter, and this astonishes me, contains only romantic arguments that seem to come out of Octave Feuillet. Nowadays—thank God!—the dilemma of *The Novel of a Poor Young Man* can be resolved fairly easily. I would only be concerned for you if you were seventeen years old and impatient.

You call yourself "a woman of the world," used to entertaining company, and in consequence, stripped of the shyness that one saw in boarding school girls in days gone by. Doesn't this acquired ease permit you to tame the nervous trembling that agitates you in the presence of your chosen one, and to engage in a conversation with him that would dissipate all your uncertainty? Since you love him, pay him the homage of your full loyalty. It seems to me you are keeping an atmosphere of confusion and reticence around your secret that can exalt your imagination, but how can real love content itself with that? In your letter I read six times words like "sadness," "suffering," and "discouragement." You should blush. Is that the vocabulary of a woman in love preparing to do battle for her love? I advise you to look at your situation with eyes that are clearer and more . . . modern. There will be time enough to tremble, to suffer, and to get discouraged if you discover that the man you love does not cherish you enough to make of you, against all the world, his wife.

Colette on Love

In this article Colette mentions Edmond About (1828–1885), a novelist and journalist. She refers at the very end of this piece to Louise de Chaulieu, one of the heroines of Honoré de Balzac's novel, *Letters of Two Brides*. This article was first published in *Marie Claire* on May 24, 1940.

It's worth quoting, the letter I received last week. But if *Marie Claire* provided hospitality for all the letters that ask it for aid or advice, in terms that are moving and often literary, each one of these bound issues would weigh as much as an epic. Luckily the letter in question can be summarized in a few words: "When the time comes, and with it old age, with what will two beings, who love one another madly, replace love?" I could answer even more briefly: "But madame, with love."

My correspondent isn't going to let me off the hook with such a brief answer. I will just let her know to begin with that I do not relish the adverb "madly," no matter where it is placed. Its vague and elastic paroxysm doesn't augur well. It's an adverb cherished by a he and she who play at being irresponsible. Turned into an adjective, it goes with every sauce: chic is mad, and the allure of a dress is mad. That hat is madly darling. I'll stop there. Why associate love with the idea of madness? To love someone is, if not reasonable, at least inescapable. You love, you are loved: that's what you need to assure the equilibrium of two entire lives, and not the brief fever of two youths. I would definitely bet that my correspondent has not reached the ripe age of thirty. She is looking from afar at that number 3 with its two bumps and it scares her. I hope that she will allow me, from the height of my two times thirty years, to try to reassure her. Does she think that love stands terror-stricken as she is by some fateful date, and that love sees that end arrive and right away withers, like a rose?

Edmond About was a very young man of letters. So young, that in one of his first comedies, where he lists on the first page the age and type of each character, he describes, "The Viscount de Sainval, pleasure seeker, age eighteen; the Baron de Réville, old and debauched, age twenty-five." Twenty-five years later, the Viscount de Sainval became, under the same pen, a "young, elegant man" of thirty-five springs, and it was the turn of the Baron de

Réville, quadragenarian, to proclaim himself a pleasure-seeker. Youth is replaced by youth. After love, reigns love, just as a prince is succeeded by a prince, his son, who resembles him.

You who love "madly," have you decided, accepted, that one day love will disappear from your life? Permit me to be astonished. You seem more resigned than a nun who, taking the veil, devotes herself to a unique and divine love. The question you pose for me, after having asked yourself the same question one hundred times, do you think that in six decades it hasn't occurred to my mind, as well? Young temple completely consecrated to one cult, will you misunderstand when I speak to you of succession and accession? It's not a question of a changing the idol. Maybe you will be lucky enough that yours will keep the same traits. It's just that the tributes you pay will be different, and marked by some chastening; we know that chastening and modesty are, for us women, almost synonymous.

From a distance and with an innocent terror, you contemplate the future of your love. Now, greedy love only sustains itself on the present. What you take for foresight is only a form of doubt. According to what happens in your letter, you can only doubt "madly," that is, by clouding the clarity of the present moment with the question of what will come later. You will quickly lose your serene countenance that way. I refer you, for further information, to Love in person, as he has been imagined and depicted in statues and paintings. When he ceases to be a mischievous child, he is a smooth-skinned adolescent, whose face only expresses a sort of radiant stupidity. Handsome young love, on whom you cruelly search for the marks of future maturity!

You can find in France, madame, many bad young marriages and many happy old marriages. Sometimes they are one and the same, as time goes by. You're smiling? You say, "Throw another log on the fire, more flames!" What? You always want to resolve all questions of love by hot and cold. If we were to believe you, the human couple can only go from fever to frostbite. You will be quite fortunate—if you have deserved it—if you traverse temperate climes. Often you will have the opportunity to wonder whether time is leading you toward your end, or taking you back to your beginnings—if you have deserved it. You don't like the word *deserve*. The feminine nature has a keen appetite for the miraculous, which is always a sort of unfair advantage and a reward for laziness. Love, a miracle strong enough to break your bones, a dazzling catastrophe, an imperious host, changes in an odd way once it takes root in a fragile earthly lodging, into a greenhouse plant that fears cold, heat, and humidity. Accept it that way. In return for that it will astonish you with its longevity.

So you don't need to hold onto the nervous fear that it will perish. One of my friends married around 1919 a "handsome chap," as people used to say, a man with a waist like a wasp, and whose thinness drove her wild. "His waist," she enthused, "is almost two inches thinner than mine." By 1940, the wasp had become a bullfinch, and we know that the puffed-up chest of a bullfinch is no small thing. What does a little puff mean to a woman who is truly smitten? When her husband gets ready to go out, my friend straightens the knot on his tie, smoothes the handkerchief in his breast pocket with a little tap, blows a mote of dust off the coarse grain of his felt hat, and tenderly watches him leave. "My dear," she says to me, "I could never stand skinny men. To me they look like a coat hanger with a jacket dangling on it, I don't know if you feel the same way."

Yes, I do feel the same way. I swear to you, Madame . . . Madame Madly. And you, too, will feel the same way she does, take it from me. That is to say, that as you continually renounce the old exaltation for a new fervor, you will reserve the severity of your judgment for yourself. Because the preservation of a work that is long, arduous, and humble—a reciprocal love—does not depend solely on the beauty of souls. Women are fond of saying that "Flirtation has no age." A great saying, but they utter it without thinking much about it. Flirtation—which is an art, a need, a pleasure—only raises itself to the level of diplomacy between the ages of forty and sixty. Afterwards, it is the instinct for dignity that adjusts and keeps in place our armor.

So many victories, madame, await you late in the day, if you neglect nothing. Pay attention to all of them. As skin loses softness, it craves finer linens. That bright color, so flattering yesterday, banish it today. Morning light—also too raw. Look up in Balzac how Louise de Chaulieu escaped the traps of the first light of day. Everything is difficult, because you are battling one opponent, daily and dear, and he knows most of your tricks. Go forth, young woman, but armed with all your weapons. What? Always these words redolent of the secret war between women and men?

Always. It's the law. Hush, now! Let's draw the shade on certain delicious antagonisms. Let's keep quiet about certain surprises that nothing should be known about, except that they sometimes place, on the face and in the eyes of a mature woman, the triumphant glow that illuminates a young bride.

Colette on Women Growing Older

At one point in her life Colette made weekly radio broadcasts, aimed at French women. Only some of the texts survive. This is the text of a talk that she delivered on July 2, 1937.

Ladies, my friends, hello. To respond in a word to your numerous letters, let me inform you that the beautiful Persian cat has found a home, friends, and a garden. But I know another cat, a Siamese, no less beautiful, young and fully grown—so, write me. This chat is already—or finally—almost a farewell. We're going to part for two months. Perhaps I'll speak to you again next Friday—but keep in mind that my mail follows me, and I hope that you won't completely abandon me. I'm going to find out, during those two months, whether you really appreciate a deep voice, diction that's only passable, and a Burgundy accent—in short, me.

But let's move on to serious subjects. I didn't expect, when I spoke last week to the listeners and correspondents who had written very moving letters, both bitter and resigned, about the sadness of growing old amidst the younger generations, side by side with their sons and daughters who are adults and adolescents, among the children of their children—I truly didn't expect that I would stir up so many agitations and recriminations. With these complaints, exaggerated or no, I notice that they almost all spring from a poisonous stream. They have their beginnings in family life. If it is easy for us to discover that our friends make up a warm family, how do we turn our family members into friends? I'm not speaking for myself, since I have—aside from my daughter—only an old bachelor brother. I know that it's a very great privilege to have had a mother like mine. She's the one who exclaimed, when I got married for the first time, "I adore you, I'm dying to see you more often, but nothing in the world could persuade me to live with my son-in-law!" She added, "And don't forget, darling, that it would be much worse if I were infatuated with your husband. A mother-in-law who doesn't like her son-in-law is normal. But a mother-in-law who cherishes her daughter's husband goes against nature, and that solves nothing—on the contrary!" She taught me that at a certain age, solitude is a sort of duty for women, a test that makes them better, and tougher. She also assured me that too much emotional outpouring is not good, because women are always having their emotional outpourings for or against someone else. Ladies, my friends: you asked me, and to respond I'm calling on the best, the most independent spirit I have known. In the village of the Loiret where she lived out the end of her life, several women of her age—and that's the age that I'm rapidly approaching—invited my mother to attend gatherings where they knitted for the poor, and discussed issues of local interest, and philanthropy. She tried it out, and came back all flustered. "I'm not setting foot there anymore," she exclaimed. "What good can come from a bunch of fussbudgets chattering away? What compassion can you expect when old women talk about the young? Phew! Enough of all those reading glasses, those needles, those crochet hooks, those whispers! Put me in front of beautiful children, kittens, birds, and flowers. And if my daughter comes to visit, tell her I'm not home, because hanging around those old biddies must have made me ugly!" When she spoke those words, she was over seventy years old.

Give me children, birds, and flowers. I know that more than one woman, old and sad, is hearing those words. Children, young animals, and flowers—that's a panacea you can't find everywhere. But if you find it, don't turn it into poison. You have to take the trouble to tame the most skittish kind of happiness, the kind that passes in front of eyes that are already dimmed, the kind that depends on getting along well with generations that are not our own. To seduce, when one is twenty, thirty, forty years old—big deal! But to seduce with hair that can no longer disguise itself, to seduce with wrinkles, to bring help and joy to those formidable opponents who are our children and grandchildren, now *that*, allow me to say, ladies and friends, is a fine piece of work, and much more worthwhile than waiting while trembling—I'm not naming anyone here!—for that inescapable and daily chime of the doorbell, than noticing that Mister Son-in-Law reserves for himself the best morsel on the serving platter, and that Baby holds her fork wrong. To suffer, yes, is proof of sensitivity, if you like. But I think there are more urgent occupations, and more honorable, than that incomparable waste of time that is called suffering.

Ladies, my friends, I'm done scolding you, and I'm sending you my very warmest wishes for a good evening.

You

This is a rare poem by Colette. She was sometimes paid to write texts that were distributed as advertisements and/or booklets by companies that marketed items such as perfumes and wines. This text was written for a company that sold women's furs. She depicts an assertive and powerful Everywoman in this poem, with capital letters reserved almost exclusively for the word "You" and its variants.

You

like a jewel
and as cold as one
You emerge as if from elemental clay
or from a museum.

with neither a necklace to play with
nor a scarf to knot
across Your flawless chest.
You wait, eyes vacant
for all that will veil you:
gems, fabrics, furs.

and your man will say, musing:
"she was naked?
I didn't realize."

I.

a beauty more slender than necessary,
thinner than they wished for,
hardly more flesh than a young Adonis,
and less hair,
receive the homage due to You.

You escape all that tradition
had in store for You.

out of prisons of marble and bronze,
outside lines painted and engraved,
outside the limits that art

assigned to You for centuries
You dash forward,
You invent yourself every hour,
You correct, with a bold hand,
the creator's handiwork,
ever-changing beauty.

II.

You declare with pride,
"I dress up for myself!"
But You lie,
it's for him that You're beautiful.

how humble You are, in the mirror,
before Your splendor!
because You guess that only one beauty counts,
the one You choose, determine, correct,
the one that demands, when You pass by,
astonishment and homage.

III.

sometimes,
You weigh down your naked shoulder
with an expanse of ermine
that equals it in whiteness.

that's how You confront, serenely,
the party nights,
the dense crowds.

You step forward, head held high,
dazzlingly bright,
wearing Your lipstick
like a flower.

don't lower Your eyes,
leave with the intoxicating certainty
that all have seen You,
and not one can forget You!

IV.

some days
You don't want any other frame, work of art,
any other case, jewel,
than the dark fur of an animal.

no one had to teach You
how to walk, lightly,
in otter, black as a Sabbath night,
the way they drape royal sable.

doesn't Your grace, on those days,
vaguely remember
when You were still a wild warrior
and naked,
fighting with other animals
for their prey, their lives,
and their skins?

V.

and what do they matter?

those lies about shape
and color
superimpose
on Your original being
another being,
gradually shaped, desired,
demanded by tenacious thought,
by a secret passion,
by a choice noble as art:
YOU

he told You, one evening
when he held You tight
in his arms
"You're so beautiful!
don't touch that face,
don't change a thing
of the gifts You had at birth!"

You smiled a smile that dazzled him,
since You smiled at Your double victory,
over him and over Yourself.

that evening, a surprising dress
clung to Your body,
a pink from a feverish flower
made Your cheek glow and Your lips,
and two long blue streaks
disguised Your eyes.

Memoirs of Friends

Portrait of Marcel Proust

Colette wrote many memoirs of her friends in the world of literature and the arts. This sketch of the great French novelist Marcel Proust (1871–1922) appeared in *Trait by Trait (Trait pour trait)* first published in 1949. Colette says she first met Proust at the salon of Madame Arman de Caillavet (1844–1910), born Léontine Lippmann to a Jewish banking family. Madame Arman de Caillavet is reputed to be one of Proust's models for the character of Madame Verdurin in his novel *In Search of Lost Time*, as well as the inspiration for two novels by her lover Anatole France: *Thaïs* and *The Red Lily*. Louis de Robert (1871–1937), who gave Colette her first book by Proust, was also a French novelist.

He was a young man during the same period when I was a young woman, and it wasn't during this period that I got to know him well. I saw Marcel Proust on Wednesdays at the home of Madame Arman de Caillavet, and his tremendous politeness was hardly to my taste, the excessive attention he devoted to those who asked him questions, above all to those females who asked him questions, an attention too clearly marked, between them and him, by their difference in age. It's that he seemed astonishingly young, younger than any other man, younger than any young woman. Large eye sockets, dark and melancholy, a complexion alternating between rosy and pale, an anxious eye; his mouth, when he was not speaking, tight and closed as if for a kiss. Ceremonially formal clothing and with a long lock of disordered hair. . . .

For many long years I stopped seeing him. I heard that he was very ill. And then one day, Louis de Robert gives me *Swann's Way*. What a conquest! The labyrinth of childhood, of adolescence opened again, explained, clear and dizzying. Everything one would have wanted to write, everything one didn't dare or know how to write, the universe reflected in a long stream, overwhelmed by its own abundance. I hope Louis de Robert knows today why he never received a thank you: I forgot about him, since I only wrote to Proust.

We exchanged letters, but I hardly saw him again more than twice during the last ten years of his life. The last time, everything about him announced, with a sort of feverish giddiness, his end. Toward the middle of the night, in the lounge of the Ritz, deserted at that hour, he received four or five friends. An otter coat, open, revealed his dress coat and white linen, his batiste tie half undone. He spoke continuously, but with some effort, his spirits gay. He kept, tilted back on his head, his top hat—because of the cold, he apologized—and a fan of hair covered his eyebrows. His every-day black-tie uniform, in short, but disheveled as if by a furious wind, which—in shoving his hat back to his nape; rumpling his linen and the ends of his restless tie; filling in with black ash the furrows of his cheeks, his eye sockets waxing hollow, and that mouth breathing haltingly—pursued this delicate young man, fifty years old, to his death.

Remembering Maurice Chevalier

This memoir of the great singer and actor Maurice Chevalier (1888–1972) was first published in *Comœdia* on September 12, 1942. Coincidentally, Chevalier later appeared in the English-language movie of *Gigi*, based on the novel by Colette. Colette also mentions Georges Wague (1874–1965) and Christine Kerf (1875–1963)—she acted in pantomimes with them. The Canebière is the main boulevard of Marseille. *Fear of the Blows* is a one-act play by Georges Courteline (1858–1929) that premiered in 1894 and depicts a couple's domestic quarrels. Mévisto the Elder (1857–1918) was a famous vaudeville entertainer. Dranem (1869–1935) was a popular comedian and café-concert singer, whose stage name is a palindrome of his real last name, Ménard.

Where did we first meet? Was it when we were on tour and took a break in the Parc de Flers, haunted by a blue peacock who refused to get mixed up with nomads like us? Was it in Lyon, in the obscure backstage corridors of that "Eden" run by a gruff man whom the performers called—not that he showed any paternal affection—"Father Rasimi." "Nobody goes on my set during the performance!" Father Rasimi said to me one day when I had come upstairs too early from those suffocating depths called the artists' dressing rooms. I answered him with one witty remark, which cost me a one hundred franc fine. No, it wasn't in the "Eden" of Lyon that I met Maurice Chevalier. Maybe in Marseille? We were making our debut, Wague, Kerf, and I, in a Crystal Palace, completely new, the paint barely dry, and the smell of plaster spoiled the perfume of the bouvardias I had bought on the Canebière. No, it was definitely not in Marseille. More likely in one of those stations where actors and singers on tour get off a train that stops at every little town, only to wait for another train that stops at every little town. It's never good, the weather at those stations. A fine, misty rain dampens the zinc roof that shelters the platforms. The first class waiting room is closed. The restaurant as well. But the refreshment stand is open. You can buy stale sandwiches there, muddy coffee, and warm beer.

I've known a fair number of train stations like that. On the other side of a bar called "The Maintenance Yard," a Terminal Hotel looked like the end of the world, and a bit beyond the station, in an open lot, stumps of bare tomato plants, linaria, and wild oats were growing. Yes, it was in this landscape striped with rails glowing with rain, between the arrival of the Achard touring company and the departure of the Baret touring company, between tinklings of the signal-boxes, that I must have met Maurice Chevalier for the first time. He was still very young—so was I. It might have been in that same station, since there hadn't been time in Paris, that I rehearsed *Fear of the Blows*. Mévisto was playing the brutal husband, so realistically that a baggage porter got angry at him.

Tall, thin, with a narrow waist, Chevalier—the crowds did not yet coaxingly call him "Maurice"—wore his unruly blond hair over his forehead, spoke little, saved his lightheartedness for the theater. Offstage, when he wasn't smiling, an intense expression invaded the blue of his pupils and he seemed like a furious child.

"See that guy over there? That's Chevalier," said Georges Wague to me. "He's gonna be bigger than any of them, even Dranem. You know what he earns, at the age of twenty?"

I indicated that I didn't and I learned to my amazement that Chevalier made one hundred and fifty francs a night. I also found out that he sent his money to his mother, except that he had bought himself a gold watch. I knew that, often, when he first got to a city, he tangled with the orchestra conductor, with the director, even with the manager, as though he only dreamt of brawls and broken contracts.

I realized soon after that even the coldest audiences couldn't resist his songs, or his acrobatic antics, or his smile.

Memories of lean times are so vivid. Many faces emerge at the slightest reminder, though thirty years have flown by. The surroundings of a station where a touring company makes a stop are not far from open country, but the countryside is inaccessible. Friendship is also not far off, but it's shy, and camaraderie imposes its own tough language.

"We've still got an hour and twenty minutes to wait. Should we go see the town?"

"To see what? Some creepy hole and the road to the station a mile away?"

"I want to sample some of the local delicacies."

"Which ones?"

"I don't know," I had to admit.

Then Georges Wague and Maurice Chevalier, accomplices for that moment, laughed at me, and Chevalier pulled out his beautiful watch one more time. He was hoping the time was passing, that the train would come, then leave, then arrive in a town where dusk would sharpen the sadness.

I believe that the period of his first success was also the time of his great misanthropy. The road, with its the rigorous solitude, its scatterings, its jolted sleep, its waking in the middle of the night, its departures in the rainy dawn, are more bitter to a young soul than to the trained and punctual barnstormer. I remember that at a railroad junction where our paths crossed, Maurice Chevalier, alone, watched us crossing the tracks. No doubt he was thinking, "Those guys, they're lucky to be a group of three." I remember he was dressed somberly and that under his fringe of sunlit hair you could see the blue of his gaze shining.

That deep azure is still shining. Tobacco smoke and harsh stage lights have not tarnished it. Loves, luck, security have softened the icy edge that glowed in it; while the unsociable, lanky boy, under a blue lantern hanging on the set supports, was waiting his turn to go on stage. He was waiting for the applause of Bordeaux, of Marseille, the pebbly explosions of laughter, the warm shouts, in short, the daily victories that turn a performer, for a few moments, into a happy man.

For a long time now Chevalier has been acclaimed, surrounded, celebrated. Has time made bland the sharp taste of that moment that throws the singer at the mercy of the public, challenging him to be victorious, one against a thousand? I don't believe it for a second. There is no artist more lucid than "Maurice." At the music hall, lucidity means modesty, secret hesitation, choice, fear alternating with the deliverance from fear, the struggle against those poor human nerves that make a hand tremble, make the knees dance uncontrollably under the pants of a tuxedo. Who knows if a corner of the mouth will start to twitch and the floodgates of a nervous sweat open wide? These little half-shipwrecks of will are more dreaded by singers than anyone else. You see in what terrible light he has to work.

One evening when Maurice was singing on the little red footbridge that leads into the theater, girds the orchestra pit, establishes direct contact between the audience and the performer, deprives the latter of the protection of the curtain, I focused my black opera glasses on this sturdy human mechanism that stood up to this magnification, this nearness, as well as a hive or an anthill projected on a screen. With a fine ear for music, the moves of a born dancer, Chevalier could have given himself over to his instinct for rhythm and seduced us as well as a song and dance act. That would have been the easy part of his mission. But with him, it's all tact and vigilance. With a healthful face that hardly needs makeup and affirms its maturity—you can't fool stage lights—he performs using all his muscles, in harmony with every expression of his body—he has the back of a hobo, the slack shoulder of a bad boy, loose knees, the facetious loins of *Prosper*—and the way he uses his eyes—let's give him his due; he makes contact every-where. "He was looking right at me, did you see?" "You think? There was a moment there where his eyes were right on me." They were both right, those two enraptured young ladies. Chevalier's precise and fleeting glance does not leave out a single spectator. Does he see them? The question doesn't even come up. What's important is that each one of us in a theater feels we've been visited. How many performers, with less mastery of a difficult art, unconsciously focus all their attention to one side of the hall? Their incomplete magnetism sometimes leaves out the right side, and sometimes the left. Or someone might fly off toward the bal-conies and warm them up, while the orchestra is left to languish. Chevalier belongs completely to all, under a pitiless spotlight that penetrates to the roughness of the skin, brings out the sweat line on the immaculate collar. Good worker of our pleasures, you are not entitled to rest or mystery—we could count your eyelashes if we wanted to. The droplet that rolls down your temple, you don't wipe it, furtively, except between two couplets, and you don't let that gesture distract us from the little comic dance step that you seem to be improvising. Your voice pierces the veil of smoke; your way of speaking that everyone envies carries your words intact and way beyond the lobby. Another evening where the public refuses to let you go, French singer in whom the Frenchman sees himself. At the end of your fifteenth song, we are finally content, your fans and I. Because I find again in your eyes that laugh at success—shh! don't mention how many years ago!—the intense and blue gaze of a young boy of days long gone.

Portrait of the Poet Léon-Paul Fargue

This is a portrait of Léon-Paul Fargue (1875–1947), a symbolist poet and essayist, and a native of Paris. Fargue wrote extensively about nocturnal explorations of Paris (like the one described in the first part of this memoir) and what he called "my secret geography." Ménilmontant is a suburb of Paris, northeast of the city, on a steep hill. Saint-Sauveur-en-Puisaye is the small town where Colette grew up in the country. Jacques Porel was a literary publisher. Goudeket is Maurice Goudeket (1889–1977), Colette's third husband. Fargue's wife, Chériane, was a portrait painter.

Nocturne

I might not recognize him if I ran into him in broad daylight. I've only seen Léon-Paul Fargue at night. Like nocturnal birds, he has vast and deep sockets, filled by the globes of his eyes. Let me remain under the illusion that he only goes out at night, and that he has the same color that clothes and protects the rat, the imponderable cat after midnight, the bat.

He is happy, after a certain hour, since I've seen him happy between eleven o'clock at night and the first light of morning. His life probably begins at the same time as the unseen toad that hangs from the sides of the steepest hills of Paris. With only a large, bold forehead and a smile glimpsed beneath the streetlamps, Léon-Paul Fargue has no more of a face than any other demon. But he is blessed, like many a demon, with a persuasive voice, with feet that climb, that cry out on gravel and cling, and he plunges into total darkness with the contentment of a swimmer. I know all this from having followed Fargue, at night, across Paris—at least he said it was Paris.

We climbed gropingly behind him on long roads, because Satan cherishes high places where he rests from the abyss. A man who came from far away and told us his name was Jacques Porel, muttered, "It's thirsty out." Right away Léon-Paul Fargue spoke to us of fresh streams, foamy beer, and promised a rest, in hopes of which we followed him without stopping until we reached a somewhat misty summit, where the fog towed along with it the smell of stables. He said, "This is Ménilmontant." We repeated, "This is Ménilmontant." But not a single one of us believed it, since we were looking for an outlying district where we would only find a village, aromas of farms, and narrow streets with sprays of lilac. I ran right into the two shafts of an unharnessed carriage, and the collision made two chickens who had roosted for the night drop right off, and they cackled. I repeated out loud, with delight, "This is Ménilmontant," and I thought to myself, "This is Saint-Sauveur-en-Puisaye."

To make the trip more amusing, our night-visioned guide then made a series of familiar wonders appear. A minuscule chalet made of wood, with semi-detached twin units, suddenly raised its Swiss-style balconies, black against a deep blue chasm, dotted with fires. "Those two little houses belong to two ladies of the night," says Léon-Paul Fargue, "and the two women are also identical. They have geraniums on the windowsills."

"How do you know?" demanded the timid voice of a pilgrim called by her companions Marie-Louise, or Bousquette.

"I feel them," responded the demon. He extended a vague arm, crumpled something invisible in the air, and the odor of a bruised geranium traveled through the night to us. A hundred steps from there a funnel-shaped coomb opened up, from which rose the stink of slime; I remember that a bit of moon polished the sides of the funnel, glossy and nauseating like the liquid edges of maelstroms. Someone barely managed to ask the name of this coomb, and Léon-Paul Fargue shook his huge head: "It has no name." One of our group broke the silence to complain about the cold, even though it was hot out, and inquired about the time. The man who called himself Porel answered, quoting Fargue, "The hour when sorrow blooms somewhere, like a petunia, for the insomniac. . . ." Immediately Fargue became agitated and uneasy, seemed to shake off an exorcism, and hurried to perform some soothing devilry, and as if by magic transported us onto the bridge over the Saint-Martin Canal, showing us that he wanted us to forget his human weaknesses, and his qualities, his vulnerabilities as a poet. But we weren't fooled, and as soon as he, with a disheartened gesture, recreated the ordinary Paris, made Ménilmontant disappear—was it really Ménilmontant?—we tucked it away between a wall and a stein of beer, somewhere on the rue de Lappe, and, reassured, we greatly enjoyed seeing him, in the light, assume the shape of a man, and under the lamplight, close his vast, wounded eyes.

The Last Soirée

Confined to our beds, we used to talk on the telephone, Fargue and I. Not that often, but at length. I loved, I still love his beautiful voice of a heavy-set man, an elastic voice, roughened by that slight suffocation that chronic bronchitis projects. My memory is my witness that we only exchanged affectionate, frivolous words, news of our work or our laziness, and, of course, our memories.

I was always curious to learn from him the way in which he suffered, his style of physical pain. "Today it's hammers, yesterday it was jaws, a sort of grinding," he said, and he asked me about my sleep, but I well understood that he was reproaching me for having unromantic illnesses. While in his mouth his sumptuous choice of words enriched his own maladies. . . . It will take me some time to be able to refer to him in the past tense.

When he granted me a spot in the upper reaches of his gallery of "Family Portraits," I had an occasion to express my joy and gratitude to him. My desire to see Fargue increased. I wanted Fargue in the flesh, Fargue crossing Lipp, Fargue wandering the streets, with his soft and indefatigable footsteps—I wanted to see Fargue. One day last summer, since I was in much less pain than he, my transportation was arranged. First in a car, across the sunset, fine weather, and the streets—the streets of Paris, the uncontested kingdom of Fargue, the dusty gold streets, their insults and their good grace—I could sense Fargue waiting for me at the end of the trip.

Rue du Montparnasse, they packed me into the service elevator spangled with coal dust. The ascension led to Fargue. Out of pride, he was already seated at the table, so I believed he might be able, at any moment, to stand up, and who knows?—maybe give me his arm to lead me to be beached at his table.

Six guests in all. But how should I count Léon-Paul Fargue, seated like Buddha, talkative and full of joy? He was generous that evening, to the point of reassuring Goudeket and me. I'm not saying he was creating an illusion for our friends, Doctor Marthe Lamy, Professor Paulette Gauthier-Villars, and Chériane herself. But he ate, scolded, laughed like an intolerant prince. He complained about the too-blue blue of the sheets, he described for us what he alone could see. He spoke to the cat, with tenderness, since the cat was glossy, as handsome and dark as Chériane. Facing me a large and strong canvas of Chériane took up as much space and presence as a guest. To my right the edge of the open window chopped off the trees at the level of their trunks: the lover of the streets lived among plane trees.

I find nothing more or less worth saying about that last soirée, to report, miss, or tenderly preserve in the friendship of our memories. Not a single one of us, not even Fargue, was brilliant. Not a single one of us needed or wanted applause, or greatness, or any special astonishment. But I know that the six guests have not forgotten a single moment, and that in our bitter certainty of not being able to do it again, we feel so destitute, loyal, and unhappy.

Cats, Dogs, and Nature

The Cat

Originally published as the preface to the book *Chats de Colette [Colette's Cats]* in 1950. The French artist Henri Rousseau painted a famous portrait said to be of the poet Pierre Loti with a cat.

There is no such thing as an ordinary cat. There are unhappy cats, cats that need to dissemble, misunderstood cats, cats who are turned over to undeserving hands because of an irreversible human error, cats that wait their entire lives for a reward that will never arrive: understanding and pity. But no amount of misery and bad luck are enough to create an ordinary cat.

Even spaying cannot eliminate the character of the domestic feline. Kiki-la-Doucette, completely neutered from an early age, only experienced a reduction in size. His liveliness remained intact and illuminated his magnificent green eyes of an alley cat, striped and with very long fur, and a little white line running down his belly. He hunted and fought; rural tomcats quickly learned to fear the strategy he devised: trapping a cat at the back of the basement, Kiki-la-Doucette leaped and fell on his enemy, soaring like a flying squirrel.

Every cat I've encountered has provided me with an example of a personal attribute, and led me to believe each time that what I was depicting was a cat that was born and lived for me alone.

From many lines, only a few pages survive. It deserved better, this animal to whom the creator gave the largest eyes, the softest coat, supremely delicate nostrils, a moving ear, paws without rivals, and the curved claw borrowed from the rosebush; the animal that is the most hunted down, the least happy, and, as Pierre Loti says, the creature most efficiently organized to suffer.

I have hardly ever stopped singing the praises of the cat. My encomiums will probably only cease with my own demise. A great wave, which has nothing to do with pusillanimous tenderness, leads me, leads me back; because cats, as a result of their predilections and loyalties, have often seemed more concerned with me that I am with them.

A Dream

Colette loved to write about dogs and cats. She devoted more than one book to her pets. A dog named Nelle, who belongs to the heroine, is a character in Colette's novel *The Vagabond*. A dog called Lola appears in her book *Music-Hall Sidelights*. Colette published this dialogue in her book *Les Vrilles de la vigne* in the revised edition issued in 1934.

(I'm dreaming. Black background smoky with gloomy blue clouds, on top of which geometric ornaments go by, each missing a fragment, either of a perfect circle, or missing one of three angles, or spirals accentuated by fire. Flowers floating without stems or leaves. Unfinished gardens; everywhere reigns the imperfection of the dream, its atmosphere of beseeching, waiting, and disbelief. No characters. Silence, then a sad, muted barking.)

ME (*startled*): Who's barking?

FEMALE DOG: Me.

ME: Who are you? A dog?

SHE: No, *the* dog.

ME: Of course, but which dog?

SHE (*suppressing a groan*): You mean there's another? When I was not yet the shadow you see before you, you just called me "the dog." I'm your dog who died.

ME: Yes, but which dog who died. Sorry.

SHE: Well, I'll forgive you, if you can guess: I'm the one who deserved to come back.

ME (*without thinking*): Oh, I know! You're Nell, who trembled as if she would die at the slightest sign of departure and separation, who lay down on the white linen in the compartment of the trunk and prayed to turn white, so I would take her without noticing. Oh, Nell! We truly deserved that one night you would finally be called back from your resting place.

(*Silence. Gloomy blue clouds continue to pass across the black background.*)

SHE (*in a voice even more faint*): I'm not Nell.

ME (*filled with remorse*): Oh, did I hurt your feelings?

SHE: Not much. Much less than you used to, when with one word, one glance, you filled me with anguish. So, maybe you didn't understand what I said: I'm *the* dog.

ME (*sudden flash*): Yes, of course! *The* dog! What was I thinking? The one where I came home and said, "Is the dog here?" As if that was your only name, as if your name wasn't Lola. The dog who always traveled with me, who knew from birth how to behave on a train, in a hotel, in a dressing room at a sleazy music hall. With your delicate muzzle turned toward the door, you waited for me. You were starving for me to come home. Bring it over here, your delicate muzzle that I can't see. Bring it here so I can touch it, I'd recognize your coat out of a hundreds. (*A long silence. A few of the flowers without stems or leaves fade.*) Where are you? Stay! Lola . . .

SHE (*in a voice that's just barely audible*): Alas, I'm not Lola!

ME (*also lowering my voice*): Are you crying?

SHE (*doing the same*): No. In the place without color where I've never stopped waiting for you, there are no more tears, you know, those tears like human weeping, that trembled on my eyes, the color of gold.

ME (*interrupting*): Gold? Wait a minute! Gold, circle of dark gold, and sparkly . . .

SHE (*sweetly*): No, stop, you're going to give me a name again that I've never heard before. And maybe far away some shadows of sleeping dogs will shudder with jealousy, will get up and scratch the back of a door that won't open for them that night. Don't look for me anymore. You'll never know why I deserved to come back. Don't grope around, with your sleeping hand, in the blue and black air that bathes me, you won't find my coat.

ME (*anxious*): Your coat . . . wheat-colored?

SHE: Shhh! I don't have a coat anymore. I'm only a line, a sinuous trace of phosphorus, a palpitation, a forgotten moan, a searcher not granted rest by death, a groaning residue, in short, of a dog among other dogs, of *the* dog.

ME (*screaming*): Stay, I know, you're . . .

(*But my scream wakes me up, dissolves the unfathomable blue and black, the unfinished gardens, creates the dawn, and scatters, forgotten, the syllables of the name carried on earth, among the ungrateful, by the dog who deserved to come back, the dog.*)

Toby-Dog and Music

Colette wrote many pieces about her bulldog she called Toby-Chien, or Toby-Dog. This one was published in the early editions of her book *Les Vrilles de la vigne* in 1908. Joseph Reinach (1856–1921) was a politician and writer, a defender of Dreyfus and a founder of the Human Rights League in France. Armande de Polignac (1876–1962) was a woman composer and musician who wrote a song cycle using texts from Chinese poems. Willy was Colette's first husband, a notorious punster. His untranslatable pun: "Nous n'irons plus hautbois," [literally: "We will go no more oboe"] is a play on a line from the fifteenth-century French children's song, "Nous n'irons plus aux bois" ["We will go no more to the woods"].

Toby-Dog, the little bulldog I was interviewing, protested, "Don't tell me I don't like music! No one really knows the true story about this, and even I myself . . ."

He interrupted his own comment and seemed lost in thought for a moment, his short chin propped up on his front legs. Three thoughtful wrinkles lined his brindled muzzle: his black and lacquered lip hung down with bitterness, and contemplating his powerfully bulging forehead, I was struck for the first time by his resemblance to Beethoven.

He reopened his batrachian eyes, and the august resemblance faded. Now, with his nostrils flaring and pulled back, the protruding globes of his eyes vaguely recalled Joseph Reinach, except more human.

"I love music," continued Toby-Dog, "because I dread it: fear is almost always love."

"Oh, most profound psychologist," I said to him, "please be so kind as to enlighten me. With what love do you surround what you refer to with such an ample and vague term: Music, all Music?"

Toby-Dog hesitated. "If I try to be precise," he admitted with charming modesty, "I'm going to stammer. You will never know how much a complicated soul like mine suffers, forced to translate his ideas with a vocabulary of a mere five hundred words. A sensitive illiterate, that's what I am, like most small bulldogs. And music increases my misery by opening in me enchanted gardens, luminous palaces, grottoes where the unfathomable trembles."

"Would you like a capital 'U' in 'Unfathomable'?" I insinuated deferentially.

"Oh, no, the usual height is sufficient. And don't keep interrupting me like that, this is already difficult enough. Music, as I was saying, is everywhere. In the raspy voice of the west wind, made husky by the rain it carries; in the icy blast out of the east that trills in the chimney, aggressive and sharp as a flute. The simmering spit of a damp log in a slow boil along the andirons mimics the fly caught in a spider web."

"Uh, excuse me, but . . ."

"The lament of the larch tree—combed by the wind—that groans, 'You're pulling my hair!' while at the very summit of its brushed-back tresses a bird whose name I don't know is calling, a bird no doubt obsessed with the memory of a vaudeville show, repeating endlessly, 'Yvette, Yvette!'"

"That's not what I . . ."

"Shall I also tell you," Toby-Dog rushes to add, "of the music of the obscure toad whose liquid note drops second by second a pearl of crystal you hear rolling between blades of grass, that freezes there? Because I believe the sparkling dewdrops have no other origin. Shall I sketch for you the kettle's shy harmonies— she's a cricket crouching in the ardent cinders, a stout little witch, benevolent, though she spits steam from her pouty lip? She is the one who sets the tempo for my sleep, interrupted twenty times, my nap in crumbs of repose that provides me no relief. Mostly she sings low; but some evenings when there is a roaring fire, she lets out a moan so sharp and so canine that her black belly makes me worry that she's eaten a lap dog alive."

Toby-Dog, out of breath, stopped for a moment and focused on me his protruding and hallucinating eyes. I took advantage of the moment to get a word in: "Excuse me, but that's not what I wanted to know about. Let's put aside natural and imitative harmonies, and give me your impression of instrumental music, even orchestras."

He became agitated, as if a sudden unease had swept over him. One of his back legs did a St. Vitus dance, gripped by a jerking motion.

"Ah, yes! I don't really like this subject of conversation. I am (as I've already said) a sensitive soul, and the very mention of certain vivid emotions is enough to make me experience them again. You saw that little convulsion I just had. I'm a little ashamed that it comes from an evening when I was listening to—entirely against my will—Madame Armande de Polignac playing the clarinet. A charming performance, I concede, with this young woman applying her naïve lips to the instrument's nasal ebony. But almost as soon as I heard the notes of the scales hatching their bubbles, scattering like round ducklings quickly taking flight, a strange fury to emulate them seized hold of me. 'Me, too!' I cried out in my thoughts. And I sang with the clarinet, and even higher than it, molding my supple voice to the congested sound of that ridiculous stick that ends with the bell of a morning glory. With my body arched like Japanese bronze dragons, with eyes bulging out of my head, and my mouth like a carp's muzzle, my expression amused Madame Armande de Polignac so much that she lost her breath and the blue of her eyes sparkled. She laughed so hard she shed diamond tears. She collapsed with mirth onto a sofa, and, with her dress thus in bloom, she resembled the fantastic butterflies that decorate the walls of her home."

"Believe me, I'm right with you."

"What difference does it make! I remain eternally misunderstood, the passionate toad through whom the soul of the panpipes is passing. Have I told you this? Major keys make me run in crazy circles, while melodies in a minor key make me pull my ears back, then my tongue turns pale and I cry out loud with I-don't-know-what inconsolable sadness. One day, at the Colonne concert, in box number 22 . . ."

"What? You follow the symphony?"

"*That's* not what I follow, it's the one who my every hour hangs upon and who took me there one day, hidden under her ample coat. Drowning in sonority, suffocating in the cascades of the harps, torn asunder by the bowstrings, while the brasses were barking at my heels, I couldn't manage a single cry, not a word, hardly a sigh, and the third act of *Parsifal* began before I could gather my wits about me."

"And so?"

"And so a luminous path suddenly parted the clouds of my foggy brain—an oboe began to sing. My will to remain silent dissolved in mysterious tears that drenched my heart. Simultaneously I felt like the most miserable and most fortunate of creatures. The sob that sprang from me was so hoarse, so incongruous, so impossible to attribute to a canine throat that as a precaution a policeman ejected from the second tier a suspicious, long-haired individual. My mistress took me home and I no longer heard the pure and frail oboe. 'Over the river and through with the woodwinds.' "

"As Willy would say."

"He probably already said it. If you would be so kind as to excuse me, now, I've waited too long to take my meditation nap. A few more moments, and it will be the time when, prim, sagacious, authoritarian, the gray female cat will arrive who reigns over this dwelling and changes, with one whap of her paw, the color of my thoughts."

The Bees of Castel-Novel

Colette's love of nature shines in these two pieces she wrote on bees. She published them in a magazine for beekeepers, *Gazette apicole*. This one appeared on Christmas day in 1923.

In the province of Limousin, at my husband's house, we only have three old wooden beehives, the old-fashioned kind, where the bees live very uncomfortably. They compensate for this in the most astonishing way. The walls of Castel-Novel are very ancient, massive, here and there crumbling: swarms find shelters inside these citadel walls that defy any attempt to reach them. The openings are extremely narrow, the bees innumerable. Their work envelops the entire dwelling in a continuous song, a golden netting, but they don't sting us. One day, while they were making repairs, they had to pull up the parquet floor of a bedroom; about ninety pounds of honey were lying underneath. It so happens that when they swarm, the bees invade one of the rooms in the chateau in enormous numbers, and for several days. We take pains not to disturb them; but the bees pay no attention to us and don't attack. I could show you, at the end of a tiny loophole, the bastions of wax of a hive inside the wall, a hive that must contain an enormous quantity of wax and honey. Our bees are not tame, but we benefit from their charmingly sociable natures. During the season when the fruit ripens they walk on my hands and face, and the wasps, too. I've only been stung once on my eyelid, by a bee that got stuck in my hair, became frightened and defended itself.

Bees

Another piece on bees that Colette published in a beekeeper's magazine, *Gazette apicole*, this one in April 1935. A bee separated from its hive cannot last long on its own.

How gentle they can be! They punished my curiosity once, I do believe. A bee, stuck in my hair that I wear curly and with bangs over my forehead, became frightened when it got caught, and left her stinger in my eyelid. But it was a case of self-defense.

The rest of the time, they are benign and patient with me. How many times in summer, in the room where I write, have I grabbed a stray bee, which was knocking against the windows to get out? I gather it up like a drop of water on the tip of my finger and say to it, "Wait, wait . . ." The miracle is that it does wait. With one of us carrying the other, we cross the room, till we get to the sunniest window. The wise bee quivers along the way, shivers its wings, unsheathes and resheathes its stiletto, just enough to touch my finger lightly with its point, just enough for me to see its hesitation, its suspicion and its peaceful thought.

On a glacial day in April that followed a few prematurely beautiful days, I found a bee on the sidewalk in Paris. It had lost all courage and was barely moving, lying on its back. I picked it up and in the hollow of my hand I "blew it warm," as children say. It began to stir in my palm and I brought it back home, where there were fire and flowers. On the corolla of a wild apple tree the bee unfolded, moved all its feet, opened its wings. But it wouldn't drink sugar water until it had completed a meticulous toilette. Its gestures, its sleeking and licking, reminded me of a cat or a bird. Then it rested, and to my untrained eye, it seemed to sleep, and dream in fits. Outside, hail was beating against the windows and spring had shut down. The worried bee, refreshed, turned toward the crepuscule its anxious antennae, its protruding eyes. I couldn't do anything for it, so I gave it death, not knowing what more beautiful gift to offer it.

Morning

This piece first appeared in the publication *Réflexions sur l'hiver [Reflections on Winter]* in 1926.

First hours of the day, the light's brief childhood, how much I already loved you when I was a little girl in the provinces. The stale air of the afternoon, hot or cold, the humdrum splendor of vertical rays, the entire human world breathes those, contemplates those. As a child, I experienced the melancholy of the daytime that bears down with the full light of a summer's day on a whole village lying prostrate, and I feared the hostility of glinting windowpanes, shut in winter from one sunset to the next.

I knew already that morning belonged to those who were willing to sink their teeth into it, and that rare are the gourmets whose passion is to sit down to eat during that part of life, that rosy hour, pearly, each time intact, each time recreated. The voice of a bird at dawn is not the same as at the peak of the day. Two wooden shoes in an empty street before dawn announce that existence is beginning again. Later in the day they are just a pair of clogs on the feet of a passerby. Suspended in the heights of fog that the morning wind breaks up, a bell tells me that the smell of warm bread is approaching, piously, on the aromatic trail blazed by the bundle of firewood lit in the hearth and the embers of the poplar in the hollow of the little stove decorated with blue faience.

So much for the lazybones who, still in bed, bolt down a lukewarm café au lait! So much for those, especially those of the feminine gender, with a sad stomach, or a sadder respect for fashion, who don't break their fast when the world is waking! The savory vapors of hot chocolate easing to a boil, and the spreading smell of freshly ground coffee that stimulates the appetite, they don't get to enjoy; or butter hardened under a pebble of ice; or grilled toast, always a little carbonized on one side. May they, these unfortunate ones, these pariahs, mourn for the tablecloth with a corny motto and garlands, and the plump coffee pot in old Paris porcelain, corseted with rosebuds! May they listen, alone with their cup of hot water, to the children with their ravenous appetites shouting on the other side of the wall, to the crackling of golden crusts, to the crystalline laughter of the sugar cubes tossed into cups! Impenitent I condemn them, these Knights of the Cracker, and with the same blow the listless sleepyheads whose night-before leads them to finish, at the stroke of noon, their evenings that began too late. "The Earth belongs to those who wake up early." The Earth? No, but the best part of the Earth, the light hour that floats above a day that's still in the making; that hour with its vapors; its red sun on the rise; its grumbling, urban language; or the rumbling of its stables, of its bees, of laying chickens; its joyful meals of milk, honey, butter, bread—delight that does not require the blood of any animal, daily feast of children and their retinue: I mean the faithful dog and the ingratiating cat.

The customs of Paris demand that between lunch and dinner served at nine, a light meal from five to six provides strength and courage to Parisians. Excuse me, but I'm not from Paris. I'm not the one to sing the praises of that bitter, black water called tea; or linens that are lacy, fringed, embroidered, or encrusted, and that fashion dictates must be slid as tablecloths or napkins, under little baskets of strawberries and slices of lemon. A snack is one thing, teatime is another, and I can't get out of my mind that in former times in my province, tea (Chinese, of course) came around nine o'clock at night to the rescue of a substantial meal.

As far as snacks are concerned, four in the afternoon—four, not five!—rang in at the same time as the end of the school day and the time "to have a little something." On the table in the garden or on the Second Empire pedestal table, depending on the season, the hemp cloth with its thick cross-stitched embroidery, spun at home, woven at a neighbor's house, embroidered at school, made the white cheese whiter, marbled with chives, flanked by delicacies like leftover beans in red wine and served cold, a cube of bacon and green pickles . . . and that's just for starters. But my elegant lady reader—weighing all of ninety-two pounds with her hat and purse—I'd bet she's choking and getting indigestion just reading this. Offended, she is going to get up and leave my rustic snack, I can sense it, for feasts more worthy of her, her eel-like slenderness, her evening dress so close—ah, me!—to actually being not a dress but a glittery loincloth. Please, madame and elegant reader, I will follow you, at a bit of a distance, and from a bit of a distance I will contemplate you, seated at a table with your guests.

Now *that*, I admire. A beautiful French table, readied for a dinner party, merits almost as much consideration as a good painting. Its traditional whiteness, gleaming in the light of an indiscreet chandelier, shines on the faces of those who surround it. The reflected light reaches the eyebrow ridges, the protruding lip, the edge of the chin, and more than one feminine beauty becomes enhanced as if she's been made up for the stage. Jeweled necklaces, pendants, bracelets, and diamonds all strike up a multiplicity of romances with the facets of cut crystal. Long, decked out in flowers, the dinner table resembles a fortunate isle, birthed by a dream, disappointing like one, since the regular ebb and flow of the somber servers who touch its shores only provide, all too often, a thin soup; a pale, translucent fish; and a cottony fowl, before the most aqueous of frozen desserts sinks and dissolves, at the bottom of the bowl, into a chemical vanilla and pinkish raspberry.

The Summer Beauty

Colette wrote this piece in 1932 not long after the designer Coco Chanel pioneered the suntan as the height of fashion. Before that, women were expected to stay out of the sun, under parasols. Colette is parodying the mania for suntans that took France by storm during this period. The 16th arrondissement is a chic neighborhood on the Right Bank in Paris. *Nigra sum, sed formosa* is from the Latin translation of the Song of Songs in the Bible, where the Shulamite says, "I'm black, but I'm beautiful," way before Martin Luther King Jr. took up the slogan. It's not known where this article was first published.

As everyone knows, the summer beauty is black. Autumn's beauty works hard to retain the beautiful colors of summer, she adds an artificial brown over a natural amber, and a cloud the color of ground coffee over everything. You would think the winter beauty has no reason to envy her predecessor, and manages so well that the December sun is astonished: "I didn't know my own strength!" Once "the holidays" have passed, that beauty reads the weather reports, packs her bags—who still uses trunks?—and leaves for the Riviera, where she leads the life of a bureaucratic nudist: morning, sun-ray treatment; afternoon, sunbathing. "It's to get ahead," explains an inhabitant of the 16th arrondissment, with Tahitian skin.

"Ahead of what?"

"When the others come back to the South of France, at Easter, I'll already be dark. I'll be at least two months ahead of them!"

A faithful attachment, a pleasure always renewed, brings me each summer, for the last seven or eight years, to the coast of Provence that a series of bad northern summers has populated and enriched. All around me that verdant zone of protection is shrinking, the oasis of little plots grown by peasants, of minuscule and deserted beaches. The summer beauty invades and exploits this serene climate with more gluttony than ingenuity. She wants everything: palazzo pants, a dress of printed muslin, and a bathing suit made of only three small triangles; a camping tent and a bathroom, aioli and minute steak, a Touareg hat and a beret, wine from Saint-Tropez, and a cocktail. The summer beauty barefoot, but in sandals with rhinestone heels.

Deep down, you don't really know what you want, beauty, or what's right to do. You follow, upheld by the great article of faith that orders you to be black, and to which you respond docilely by shaking your little bottle of suntan lotion: *"Nigra sum."* Sed *formosa*? That's another matter altogether. Not everyone can be a Shulamite, and often your novitiate causes me quite a bit of grief. And I still don't understand why you want to be so black.

At the back of my garden in Provence the sea has scooped out a little cove. The place is so private that the blue gurnard, if it flies off the sea and plummets onto the beach, risks dying there without hope of rescue, and without anyone being the better for it. A young woman, two years ago, got it into her head that my little cove and its curtain of tamarisk and pine lent itself to a "sun cure," as they say. She arrived around ten in the morning carrying her robe, a beach umbrella, and a little basket of fruit, and let her palazzo pants fall to her feet. Her beach umbrella deployed, the young woman was not at all embarrassed by my presence. Her bathing outfit followed the pants, and the ceremony began. Cook the front, cook the back. Maybe a quick dip, but not essential. Drying. Cook the front, cook the back. Quick dip, etc. Eleven o'clock. Noon. The sun reached the peak of the sky, pouring onto the sizzling sand, onto the exhausted sea, and onto the voluntary victim of Moloch, that triumphant, unbearable heat, which makes, in contrast, the shade seem so cool.

Around one o'clock, the poor young woman put back on her light clothing and sandals, ate a few morsels of fruit, and left with shaky footsteps. Faithful to the rite, she started again in the afternoon. Each day she got darker, thinner, more wobbly, and sadder.

From July 1 to August 15, blue trains, green trains, cars of every make pour onto our Provençal coast a daily dose of families, more or less northern, who reject all clothing as soon as they set foot in our treacherous and heady South of France. Wearing just their underwear, the children bare their bodies to the salt and flame. Neither one nor the other takes pity on them, and they have no defense against deep burns. Summer beauty, you don't always forget to be maternal, and your fate, to begin with, is no better fate than your progeny's. I remember two terrible years, where bandages were the height of summer fashion. We would say, "I saw that woman with both her arms wrapped in gauze." "The little girl with the scarf of liniment looked really grouchy this morning." "Have you seen that pretty blond with a collar of burns? She worked up a white and red outfit, with shantung pants, a scarlet hat, a handkerchief like a corsage over her breasts, and starch powder in the shape of a cape over crimson shoulder blades: gorgeous!"

But humor never solves anything. Dear summer beauty, since you cling to this land of mine—I consider it my own with the fierceness of a former invader, or a communist citizen promoted to border guard—know at least how to make use of it and try to find some sort of compromise. Isn't it because I was thinking of you, of your sensitive skin, of your overwrought nerves, that I conducted tests, pored over the doses, and filtered my oils, my cooling lotions and my protective unguents? I dedicate them to you.

And don't play with the powers that rule the capricious South of France. If you leave your bed early, you'll learn that the dawn is streaming with dew and blessings. But cover yourself in the middle of the day and keep your children in the shade as well. Banish strong liquor, drink young wine, walk in the open air, play in the sunshine, don't lay in it too long. That's how I've fashioned myself, for the last seven or eight years, to live during summer on one of the most beautiful coasts in the world, having learned from this person or that, from a neighbor, from a bird, from a storm, and from a shift in the wind. The first year I came to Provence, we harvested our grapes under the flames of August—you tell me if the vines were in a hurry! In my little vineyard, as long as the sun was low, I saw nothing unusual about the women harvesters. But at the stroke of nine o'clock, my wise Provençal women put down their baskets and scissors for a moment; they covered their heads with their wide-brimmed hats, rolled their sleeves right down to their fists, tied scarves around their necks, and then the two youngest women put on gloves.

Snowdrop

Colette first published this piece in *Mélanges*, a collection of essays she wrote at the end of her life. In nature the stem of the snowdrop bends over, letting its flowers dangle down. The snowdrop is also one of the first flowers to bloom in the spring.

If a bee had three wings, it would be a snowdrop. Or, to rephrase: if a snowdrop only had two wings, would it be a bee? This is where my reveries go when they escape from a painful arthritis attack, free to wander. A bunch of snowdrops is steeping in a glass of water next to me, on a coffee table. They are the first of the year, but they move me far less than the spur of the first violet, the hyacinth's horn, the valve of the lily of the valley. Because the custom in Paris is to meddle so the snowdrop buds are gathered and assembled into tight clusters, forcibly raising its fragile closed calyx, paralyzing it without hope of blossoming, against the inclination of the flower. How, in this frustrated bouquet, in this imploring and vertical posture of so many creatures, where the florist has contradicted its essential wish, how to recognize my bee with its triple wings, my drooping teardrop pendent, the "dangling earrings" of my childhood, its tightly fitting green bodice, its white skirt smoothed by a breath, loosened as early as January. In Paris they don't know its true dimensions and its secret, the chaste white petticoat underneath with its six teeth, short, candy-striped in vibrant green. Does Paris even know that, thriving and free, in the middle of the day the snowdrop exhales a breath like an orange blossom?

I unbound them, immersed the stifled flowers—I'm waiting for them to resume their normal pose, for them to lower and shake their heads of tintinnabulating flowers. In vain. Some succeed, lean over, then succumb. I'm only giving them the chance to interrupt the strain imposed on them, and to die graciously.

War and Peace

Their Letters

Throughout her career Colette published articles in newspapers and magazines on a variety of topics, including current events, fashion, and her childhood. In the heat of World War I, she wrote this homage to letters sent from the trenches by soldiers. It contains a remarkable acknowledgment of the humanity of a soldier fighting on the other side, for Germany. The Lorraine is one of two provinces of France that Germany partially annexed in the Franco-Prussian War, and that France reclaimed after World War I. *The Songs of Bilitis* is a book of erotic poems by Pierre Louÿs (1870–1925), set to music by Debussy. This article was first printed in *La Vie parisienne* on January 30, 1915.

Their letters . . . They travel slowly, stop, end up getting lost. But those that complete their journey reveal the pleasure of, and the thirst for, writing that guides the pens of our soldiers, on whatever sheet of paper they could lay their hands on. Never before has France written so much. Even after the letter of a father, son, or lover, the letter more urgent than air or bread that cries out to his loved ones, "I'm safe," he *still* writes. He confides in friends he doesn't know, and almost apologizes: "It's because of an article in an old newspaper that I thought of writing to you."

It's worth keeping a record of the pages that follow this timid beginning, four pages of confidences and wildness, with the expansiveness of a schoolboy, memories of adolescence, accounts of battles, nostalgia for beloved books, a long reverie under the stars where the heavy pulse of the canon is beating, then an awkward and stiff closing—and no signature. Ten letters resemble that one, in their anonymity, the mix of abandon and ceremonious reserve: one contained a little anthemis flower, picked at the outside edge of a trench, a bloom that hadn't yet lost its bitter perfume of chamomile. They are so much like brothers, these Frenchmen smitten with books and newspapers, respectful of the printed word! One of them, for four months, adds a full kilo to his pack rather than leave behind four cherished volumes. Where is he right now, that muddy, sentimental, and cheerful bibliophile? What remains of the group who joined with him: "two students of the National School of Paleography and Archival Studies, who like to stump us with questions and scrounge tobacco; a cubist painter who sees the war in episcopal purple and black; a wine merchant, delicate and poetic, who knows *The Songs of Bilitis* by heart; a pharmacist renowned for bleeding chickens and skinning rabbits; a coffee planter who has hunted tigers; a pianist; a cotton broker"? "When night has fallen and the canons go silent, we collapse with fatigue, and right away we start to talk about our work, impressions, memories, books, to prove that we're still alive, that we exist very strongly. If there's wine, we raise our mugs and say, 'Here's to the health of those having less fun than we are, in Paris! To the memory of those kicking the bucket near here, while we wait our turn! To the Lorraine, which we're keeping!' And then we lay down on the ground and we go to sleep."

"We go to sleep. . . ." Confident youth sleeping on the ground, a fine people, intoxicated with dying for an idea—but the most beautiful of all ideas!—yet you are concerned about disappearing altogether, and you save from the fire, to throw them to us before going to your fate, your last thoughts, with the last flower on the slope!

But I hunt in vain for signatures—those who write feel rich enough to give, without asking anything in return. One might say that these brave men are only stirred by their consciences, and tremble only at judging themselves. Delicacy, compassion, I'm searching for a word that is worthy of the gesture of that national security agent, whose name we will never know. He received, for a wounded German, a little Christmas package: a wool scarf, a little piece of chocolate, and two small branches of green pine, come from so far·away and so slowly that the wounded man did not have time, before dying, to hug the rough greenery.

But the officer looked for and found his grave, to give back to the dead his due, his most precious and last possession: the green memory of his snowy province in Germany.

In the Home for Blind Soldiers

In this piece, Colette pays close and compassionate attention to the losses of World War I, the first war that entailed casualties in the millions caused by modern weapons. *Letters from My Mill* is a collection of short stories by Alphonse Daudet. This piece was published during the war in the newspaper *Le Matin* on April 21, 1915.

Yesterday military medals were conferred on three heroes, struck by blindness in the course of duty.

The former convent of the Sisters of Saint Catherine shelters, behind its black façade devoid of beauty, those struck with blindness by shrapnel or the explosion of a shell.

A severe, narrow door, below the banner *Convalescent Home*, half-opens: it's the light, the perfumes of a deep garden, the sky of an orchard dappled with white trees; it's a snatch of music made up of the songs of blackbirds and a chorus of untrained and joyful voices, led by a piano. The surprise is so gentle, so poignant that one doesn't dare speak. The hospital for blind soldiers is holding a celebration today for its three most recent medal recipients.

They are all there, about fifty of them, in the first rows; and a very small but friendly crowd. Their faces without eyes, raised toward the podium, listen to the speech of a director who is having a difficult time speaking. They seek out the three comrades being honored, three terribly pale soldiers, who sob when the medals are pinned on their chests. But they don't start crying, as a group, until the moment when "The Marseillaise," too grand for this narrow hall, resonates to make the walls burst. We wouldn't know they were crying except for the convulsions that make their mouths tremble, except for the shaking of their hands, leaning on canes, since there are many here who can no longer shed tears.

Afterward I leave them to their refreshments in the garden, to the glass of champagne, toward which, greedy as children, they hurry on the arms of their nurses. I actually saw them better the night before, alone, in their home, with their everyday expressions, their thoughtful faces with shut eyelids. They dazzled me with their wisdom, their joy, their thirst for life. I was able to move about without being seen, but not without being sensed, by the one who was punching in Braille *Letters from My Mill*; to the one finishing his first brush, and who cried while he pressed the hands of the director, who was deeply moved, "Monsieur, monsieur, I'm saved! Monsieur, I can work, think of it, I can *do* something! Monsieur, it's going to be all right, it's going to be all right!"

The man who was writing in white on white, his first book, smiled from ear to ear while applauding: "Can you believe how quickly I'm learning!" And another blind soldier, whom I wanted to buy a brush from, took offense: "Who do you think I am? No, no, don't offer me money."

"But I wanted . . ."

"Yeah, you wanted to do an exchange, I understand, you want to be nice to me. Then give me—if it's not too much trouble—give me a little bouquet, to put at the head of my bed."

"What kind of flowers would you like? Flowers that smell nice?"

"If it's not too much trouble, I'd like some *yellow* daisies. Some beautiful *yellow* daisies. Now, that's pretty."

I watched them for a long time. Even those who have been here since September do not walk anything like those born blind. The mutilated are naturally less adroit, more awkward. They bang into walls, into furniture, and sometimes get impatient: but what a difference between their gestures and the sort of sleepwalking safety that guides those born blind! Our wounded keep, will always keep, under their two scars that still burn, the memory—magnificent, colored, precise—of the world they live in, its dimensions are known to them; space, the nuances, distances, will never be for them meaningless lessons. The memory of having seen makes easy the simple crafts that will become a livelihood for them.

"If you could only see," says the director of the hospital to me, "how quickly they're progressing! Brush-making, basket-weaving, gardening, carpentry, they can learn anything they want. They astonish me each and every day. They don't have the fearful and complicated mental state of many people who are born blind. Mine [*sic*] are not crippled, they are men, real men, stopped by a cruel wound . . . for a while. And if you knew the touching thought that motivates almost all of them: the hope of marriage, the hope, above all, of love. I'll get them married, you'll see. We've already had engagements here. I will get as many of them married as possible. They are so sweet, so brave, so loving. They are so . . ."

He searched for a word, extending his arms, and his hand was grabbed in its motion, and held by two affectionate hands, the two divining hands of a blind person: "They are . . . ah, they are passionate!"

The Eyes of the Dragonfly

This is another piece Colette wrote during World War I. She turns to the most disheartening scenes of trench warfare and finds that vitality, compassion, and amazement can still persist in the most unlikely places. Le-Mort-Homme (literally: "The Dead Man") was a famous battlefield in more than one war, synonymous with hell on earth. Professor Perrier could be either of two brothers, both French zoologists: Edmond Perrier (1844–1921), or Rémy Perrier (1861–1936). The Meuse River in the province of the Lorraine was the site of the some of the worst fighting in World War I. First published in *Excelsior* on January 29, 1918.

"Do you know that in a passage between trenches on the right bank of the Yser, six meters behind one of the four guns of the 9th battery while it was firing, in a little cavity of sand, they found . . ."

"The plan for a coup d'état? I would've bet on that."

"And you would've lost your bet. This find, by the way, goes back to last May. They found a nest of very tiny birds, wheatears, who fed and raised their young through the daily blasts of the guns. Also, in the same region, there was a nest of magpies in an isolated elm tree that was used for target sighting by several batteries. In that ghost town called Le-Mort-Homme, a quail was so indifferent to the bombardment that she never stopped singing on the parapet of the trenches. She built her nest at the foot of it, in a little fold of the prairie."

I find this out from soldiers, officers, who have seen it with their own eyes, who report it to Count Tristan, to Professor Perrier, and to their good friends. A sergeant major at the front describes, in loving detail, the gestures of a wagtail bird, hunting insects around the trenches. For the rest, read the newsletter published by the League for the Protection of Birds: there you can read the story of a couple of starlings who fed a beakful to a squawking brood in a nest attached to a section of a ruin that was still smoking. Imagine, near the Meuse River, as night descends, at the hour when silence falls over the canons, machine guns, and grenades, imagine the voice of a nightingale singing, moved only by the approach of night and love. You read the story of the swallows of Fleury, who warbled confidently among our soldiers, at the thundering minute of the attack.

Read, smile, be moved by it. You will murmur, "That's wonderful." Yes. It's wonderful that the eyes of man have seen, recorded these things, have acquired, with regard to tiny creatures, a consideration that will endure. So these eyes were not blinded by canon fire, nor crushed by the approach of the darkness where so many young bodies have gone cold forever? Because it's not at all a question of files compiled by a dispassionate and professional eye. The astonishment, the delicacy, the poetry that appears in these notes brings them to life. They were gathered by new eyes, open since the war and by the war, eyes astounded by a cricket in the roof thatching, dazzled by a lark, the dew, the dawn—scales fall off their eyes, in fact, won over, in contemplating death, by gratitude, by the respect for all living things. Eyes for whom the horizon is a slope pockmarked by bullets, a wall of mud, a canopy of branches, a narrow swatch of sky churning with murderous stars, what a peaceful light you still cast on the overlooked nest, flower, or insect.

An officer, whom we pressed to paint a picture of the trenches, the attacks, his life in combat, kept coming back to the same detail: "There was a kitten in our shelter, a little black kitten that we found. You can't imagine . . ."

"Yes, yes, we can imagine. But it's not the cat we're interested in."

"Really?" The officer was astonished. "I'm interested. I had no idea what a kitten was like."

I remember a summer day before the war, when I met in the countryside one of those men, rare in any land, who completely deserve the name, so disparaged these days, of a "person of note." I had caught a large dragonfly, malachite, turquoise, gauze, and mother-of-pearl, and I showed it to him. This eminent man gave it a look, and a predictable comment: "Very pretty."

Then he started to pay attention, pointed to part of the creature: the eyes, the enormous eyes, those two iridescent globes, unfathomable, those jewels where reflections played, reflections of water and azure, all the colors of the universe.

"What *is* that?"

"That? Those are just its eyes. . . ."

He leaned over, gazed passionately: "Its eyes? Are you sure? Do you mean that all dragonflies have eyes like that? It seems to me I would have seen them before, wouldn't I? Its eyes."

He took the creature, touched it lightly with his hand, and when he gave it back to me, murmured to himself: "Look at that. Things like that exist, and we don't even know. We have to tell

people about it, we have to let people know about these eyes. . . ."
The fervor, the wonder of the discovery appeared on his face, so new and so gentle, and so communicative, that I truly had the impression that he was the one who had just invented, to bequeath them to the world, the eyes of the dragonfly.

Colette Speaks to Americans

Colette delivered this radio address in January 1940, when France was fighting Germany in World War II. This was before the attack on Pearl Harbor in December 1941 when the United States entered the war, and before the collapse of France's defensive barrier, the Maginot Line, which led to surrender. In this radio program, Colette presents French soldiers as sensitive and feeling individuals, worthy of the support of their North American brothers. Beneath the lyrical details, Colette creates a well-thought-out appeal for the U.S. to support France in the war, which it ultimately did, but not until the D-Day invasion four years later.

I'm not absolutely sure that my listeners and my American friends will be very curious about what I have in front of me on my work table. It depends on the curiosity and the interest that I inspire in them. If they knew me better, if they had some affection for me, I would have no problem making them curious about whatever is around me. Perhaps we will get to that point. But it's too soon to think about that. If I spoke to you about my daughter's photography and about my work habits, you would shut off the radio or maybe you would replace me with some good music, and you would be exactly right. But I think that, if what I'm saying touches, in whatever way, on this war that the entire world is suffocating from, you will listen to me. So: on my work table I've kept, since the month of October, a little pen-and-ink drawing that means a lot to me, a drawing of a grasshopper.

It's not the work of a master. But it came to me accompanied by a charming letter from a young and unknown soldier. It's a moment that is not disagreeable in the life of a woman, the moment when the "confidential letter" takes the place of the love letter. My young artist confides in me that before being sent to the front, he completed a period of military training in the radiant South of France. And he adds that he can't completely curse this war, because without it he would never have known what's outside a big city, geometric and dark, an industrial city, black with plumes of smoke. He writes to me that before becoming a soldier he had never seen sprouting grass, or the last roses, or an animal in the wild, or the flight of wide-winged birds over the sea. He writes to me that he's in the South of France, near the sea, and that he sees all around him the miraculous world, with the eyes of a child to whom life, up till now, had refused everything. The proof that he's sincere is this grasshopper that he drew in pen in the most minute detail, with the wonder, the strict observation of nature that characterizes certain Chinese drawings.

His model, which I know well, is one of the larger grasshoppers, green as a peapod, which in Provence in the South of France flies off suddenly, gets caught in muslin curtains, and thrashes around with a noise like a battery-operated toy, and nips your finger very sharply with two keen-edged mandibles if you try to free it. They have a big horse-like head with an aquiline nose, take up as much space in the air as a swallow, and make as much noise as an airplane.

If I keep going on about this creature, I don't know how I'm going to stop, I'm so amazed. But it's easy to see that my young portraitist of the grasshopper is as amazed as I am. "They tell me," he writes in his letter, "that it's a grasshopper." And he notes very respectfully under the insect, "Grasshopper." This little drawing leaves nothing out. The long wings of gauze have their veins, the large feet of the grasshopper are accurate, outfitted with imperceptible clamps, and little hooks that serve as fingers. And the grasshopper's large oval eye, a pale green convex mirror that reflects the universe, seems to be looking at me sideways. The bark of the tree on which it sits I also recognize: cracked, gnarly, like the crust of a planet seen through a telescope—it's the bark of a tree that yields delicious oil, the bark of an old olive tree.

That's the drawing, the fruit of three days of observing and admiring, three days of discovery, made by a young French soldier, before throwing himself into a setting where there are no grasshoppers or olive trees with silvery leaves. I know you won't make fun of him, young men of America who carry in you, just as he does, the love of observing nature and animals. I know you will think about this child of the city, who, dazzled and intelligent, never had the opportunity to lift his gaze and see the infinite and multicolored page of nature, the wonders that it puts within reach of our hands, as numerous as the stars, the grass, and the days of heaven.

He's not the only one, my portraitist of the grasshopper, to attest that war, far from taking the bloom off our species' delicate capacity for noticing and observing, refines and expands it. I have other letters besides his, other revelations, other astonishments in addition to his. The mothers, the young wives of the soldiers need not fear that life at the front will change the handsome sons of France into brutal champions. I would think the contrary would be the case. If at this moment, many of them are disguising their youth with a closely cropped beard, sported by infantry sappers during the Second Empire, that doesn't make them insensitive or crude. The tough school of shared risks also involves turning inward, and melancholy. I visit, during their leaves, a handful of men. From those men in the armed services, I receive a relatively small number of letters. When they're around me, these men on leave put on a show to appear jolly out of manly pride, partly because they feel obligated to resemble the idea we've formed of them. But when they're far away and they write to us, they confide more in their letters than in what they say out loud. The most revealing confidences come from total strangers. They write to me simply because they know my name, or remember something they read. What light they shed, those letters, on the traits that the French national character can legitimately claim! Emboldened by distance, or by anonymity, their authors give in to the need to talk, to the desire to be understood, to the thirst for replacing the tired or gross phrases of contemporary language with a word that's slightly more elevated, with a poetic image; to surrender, for a moment or for an hour, the guarded stance that forces almost all of them to make fun of themselves. Those are the main causes that give rise to such lovely letters, letters that are truer than everyday life. Our heritage is good. I think I know it fairly well, simply because I've had the time to get to know it and the desire to observe it. Bad little jokes, the famous French "jests"—I detest that word, "jest"—just hide what is best in it and in particular the poetic impulse, the reaching out for lyricism, that lies in wait for us around the age of fifteen. Here's an example: I continually receive literary essays, prose, and verse. The beginning prose writers sign their essays with their names and give their addresses. While a poet, male or female adolescent, immediately puts on the disguise of a pen name, a beautiful, mysterious, and childish name, the name of a celestial star, or a romantic hero. That choice itself is a poem.

But war is a huge torrent—unfortunately tainted with precious young blood—an enormous wave that drowns all the bad little jokes made out of embarrassment, and that drowns petty pride. In wartime, a man who's been a husband many years no longer hesitates to write to his wife the letters of a passionate lover, and doesn't hesitate to risk his life to save a comrade he didn't know the day before. A man at war, a Frenchman at war, is lavish with his heart. They are forever, even at twenty-five years remove, inseparable brothers, my young military man with his grasshopper, and the soldier of the trenches who, in 1916, sent me a little yellow flower that escaped trampling, a survivor of a clay trench, with these words of a poet: "I'm sending this to you," he wrote, "because I looked at it so long it became a gift." That man with the yellow flower, the man with the grasshopper, aren't they also related to my young doctor friend, too young to have fought in the last war, too much a man of science to have loved his peers up till now except in a form torn apart, deformed by illness, too preoccupied to allow himself the luxury of an emotional friendship. This very young man of learning has just left, his first leave finished, for a "somewhere in France," in an unfortunate location. When he left, he looked like a Christmas tree, all hung with thermoses to hold hot coffee for his men, iron kettles for the toddies of his men, raspberry brandy for when his men get the blues, aspirin for the colds of his men. And he also carried boxes of powdered milk for a four-month-old puppy that he found on the front during God-knows-what solitude and misery. This handsome young man, cold before the war, discovered in the war, helter-skelter: friendship, compassion, universal tenderness. I wanted to laugh at him, naturally—that awful obsession we have for ridiculing what we admire—but couldn't, it's so astonishing and . . . respectable, yes, respectable, that honeymoon of a young man and the human species, that terrific guy who was breaking through the windows of his greenhouse to put out branches in every direction. But since he's a doctor, he knows nothing, absolutely nothing, about how to raise a four-month-old puppy. I recovered at the same time as my composure a bit of our very French irony, and for his little dog I wrote him out a prescription.

Parisians Go on Vacation—To Paris

Written during the German occupation of France, this piece begins with a lovely but fairly innocuous description of the pleasures of staying in Paris during the summer, a situation necessitated by World War II. The location is the butte of Montmartre. Colette criticizes the Nazi occupation by satirizing the Germans' decisions to switch Paris to Berlin time (two hours later) and to outlaw parakeets and other pet birds. This article by Colette was first published in *Le Petit Parisien* on June 26, 1941. Cardinal Richelieu was responsible for increasing the gardens in Paris by first building part of the Palais-Royal, with its internal courtyard, now a public park, and also the building where Colette had her apartment then. Terpsichore is the Greek muse of dance, who inspired the Duncans, Isadora and her brother Raymond. The Countess de Sérizy is a character in Honoré de Balzac's novel *Scenes from a Courtesan's Life*.

"What time is it?"
   "Twenty-one o'clock."
   "Oh, right, nine o'clock."
   "Oh, right, seven o'clock."
   We are all correct. The garden is still open, with kids scattered all over. The birds, the animals in their homes, and the children all function on solar time. And the latter refuse to go to bed before the sun, which is using the balconies to create on the ground a horizontal and yellow border, an afternoon and midsummer border. In vain they shout at the little girl flitting about, "Come on, Yvonne! You won't get to bed before ten, that's grown-up time!" She persists in running in zigzags, under the network of swallows. Children don't move in a straight line any more than swallows do. With the swallows, it's easy to explain: they're hunting. Also children. But they won't tell us later what they were pursuing on their broken paths, because they will have forgotten. One door cannot open in front of us until another shuts behind us.
   Through some maternal trick the little girl is finally captured. I imagine that this little girl, for the entire summer, will not have any other beach, any other forest than the space provided by Cardinal Richelieu and the Tuileries Gardens. Many children won't leave Paris. With low levels of smoke, purged for a while of gasoline fumes and a good part of its dust, let's say that Paris is—and I'm going to find this out for myself—very livable. Its well-planted avenues, its public gardens have destined it to have a population that stays put, and is content to do so. No other capital has so

many private gardens. So often a tiny and secret oasis, enclosing a tree carded by a cat's claws; a grassy islet; the shaded lily of the valley; lilacs . . . Right in the center of town, fairly recently, the demolition of the wall of a building revealed to the passerby the presence, beyond two deep courtyards, of a mossy flight of stairs; a cluster of trees; a long, flowering stem of digitalis; and a regal cat. In the 16th Arrondissement, it wasn't until a pickax and a trowel moved in that I discovered, behind a lovely porte-cochère, an Eden of apple trees all in a row, rosebushes, and cabbages, and on the domes of the bell jars sparkled stars of sunlight.

It's one of the adventures of Paris to land up on the slope of the butte, as I did this week at the end of a cul-de-sac, among the privets, ivy, and rosebushes clinging to the steep incline. Once you cross the threshold, you are in the middle of a terraced garden, by the side of a shaded swimming pool, under the chestnut trees and the acacias. A sort of feminine kindness embraces the children of Paris here, a kindness it offers seminude to the sun, the clear water, and the free-flowing Terpsichore who inspired the Duncans.

Above the swimming pool and solarium, the eye ascends again to gardens, a balustrade marked by urns of flowers, dreamers leaning on their elbows, a hedgerow that reveals a villa, the shaded remains of a provincial Paris. At several levels of the foliage, children in bloom incline—they're not too noisy, just disciplined enough. A fifteen-year-old girl jumps into the cool water, reaches out her hands to a little girl of five, and a six-year-old duck follows them. Here, 97 degrees in the shade is not a problem.

There are days when, because of the pure light, the season in its full brilliance, all happiness seems in reach. I would like, for everything Paris possesses that is most delicate and precious, protected enclosures. Paris vacations exist thanks to a few people of goodwill, provided that the city does not leave its children without volunteers to watch them, amid the dryness that makes Paris swoon, in July and August, like a city devastated by fire. Why, for more than a year now, in the middle of the Palais-Royal, has our large mirror of water dried up? Around it the air was cooler, and its clement moisture left pearls on the grass. Air, water, leaves! No other capital had, in former times, as many gardens, no other one hid them as jealously. When I flew over it at a low altitude, I was surprised at the number of these private, tiny, unexpected, pampered gardens.

All the children of the garden have now gone home. But the days are so long that the parakeet cage is still chattering.

Tomorrow it will chatter no more, since a "Regulation" took note of its presence and is banning it. It wasn't any more of a nuisance than a bouquet of flowers. Blue parakeets, green parakeets, scarlet tanagers, who were you offending? The Regulation. Two little green cases that decorated a doorstep under the arcades had to go, for the same reason. Flowers, mottled wings, chirpings, back to the shadows! Respect The Regulation that watches, unmoved, as wars pass by and the shapes of nations change!

Yet Balzac tells us how the Countess de Sérizy, when she wants to prove that a handsome suspect is innocent, treats a certain bit of legal red tape, which she pries out of powerful hands and tosses in the fire. I'll stop there, on my way to becoming the only seditious citizen of the Palais-Royal. Monsieur the Director of Fine Arts, I'll stop now, continuing to hope that a wave of your hand will, if not open the cages of the parakeets, at least liberate the spirit of our huge spray of water, that handsome liquid feather divided into twelve foamy plumes, where rainbows play, and where birds bathe in mid-flight.

The Writing Life

Ways of Writing

This personal essay spans numerous topics, from Colette's writing implements, to her thoughts on handwriting analysis, to recollections of the first love letters she wrote and received. Jules Crépieux-Jamin (1859–1940) was one of the first French graphologists, or handwriting specialists. In 1897 he was asked during a critical moment in the Dreyfus case to give an expert opinion on whether the handwriting of the compromising memo was in Dreyfus's hand, and he said it was not. The original date and place of publication of Colette's essay are unknown. Reprinted in *Cahiers Colette* No. 2, 1980.

"How many do you have? Seven! One for every day of the week? Seven pens? That's a fortune!"

If seven pens constitute "a fortune," it's not of the *nouvelle riche* kind. The newest one has ten years of service; as for the oldest, we first came to an understanding around the year 1920. It definitely looks its age: it's made of mottled, old black mahogany; but this pen is a marvel, one of those helpers that a writer only finds two or three times in an entire career. Stocky, but at the same time flexible, with a wide nib, but capable of delicate strokes and not blinding the letter *e*, I have only known one to rival it, and that pen died in the line of duty.

Just as a horse at the end of its service lacks the use of all four legs and can no longer stand up, this irreproachable pen broke in the course of its labors—its two points flew up at my nose: it performed its duty from February 1909 to May 1925—you see that I've bookended its dates to memorialize it, with justifiable gratitude.

The first fountain pen that fell into my hands took me a long time to love. The capillary action of its cartridge deprived me of an essential piece of equipment—the little watering trough of ink, called unspillable, but easily knocked over. It was a gesture like breathing, the to and fro of the thirsty pen pointing toward the well its nib shaped like the diminutive beak of a ring dove.

My seven pens stand at the ready, all different, in a little blue faience pot. They take turns, each one having its particular task and merits.

A marbled skinny one is restricted to correcting proofs. It's frail, armed with a point that's too sharp. But its double nib excels at insinuating itself between typographic figures, accurately traces the deletions, treads lightly over the spongy paper of galley proofs. I am not at all attached to this honest servant, but I'm very happy to find him when I need him.

Plump, yellow as a chick, robust, with black edges, not much personality—another serves as my work horse, good for long hauls. It knows how to copy, rewrite, and its ample marks please the typist.

A fountain pen of the fancy kind, decked in silver, comes from far away, souvenir of a Brazilian journalist. It's as capricious as a barometer, but soft to the touch, curve-friendly, the one that helps me with difficult projects.

Of my two North American twins, I have only good things to say.

How little room it takes up, the writer's toolbox! Do so many blackened pages leave me, if not proud, at least with the slightly bitter delight that certain privileged people taste when they succeed at their task and then contemplate it? I wouldn't dare to claim that, for the good reason that I don't know how to contemplate my own work. I forget it, so it doesn't weigh me down. Isn't this the fate of writers for whom patience replaced a fiery calling? In those days, that great revealer, love, did not draw out from a young girl of sixteen the first fruits, the lights, the inspired sorrows that might rescue and warn her.

Sixteen years, a happy life in the bosom of the village where I was born, the most trusting parents . . . Love riled much that had been transparent, and love, even confused, cannot dispense with writing. Respect for the truth obliges me to admit that my maiden letters did not herald my career as a writer. They were limited by my shyness, preoccupied as I was with keeping my writing proper, to decorate my capital Gs (my first name is Gabrielle) and the M, almost Gothic, of the first line: "My darling." A certain distinguished gray-blue paper seemed to me the only one worthy of my amorous, and, of course, clandestine correspondence. Where to hide so I could write? Not in the room I had occupied since childhood—my mother's room had a commanding view of it. Our library was not a possibility, where our friends from the village came to consult my father's fat Larousse dictionary and swarmed like bees on a trove of fruit! From a romantic standpoint, for the pounding of a young heart, and for lies—the place I chose was a hundred times better. Along a road, midway between the train station and our small market town, a bench, almost always empty, was my accomplice. Seated on the ground, with my legs extended under the bench that I used as a desk, I wrote. Not a thing was lacking from the moving banality of the décor, not the double hedge of hawthorn, not the pleasant curve of the road squeezed between its grassy borders, not at times the unforeseen passerby from whom I fiercely hid my letter. I wrote. "My dearest dear one, I couldn't shut my eyes for one minute last night, you were both too near and too far. And besides, I'm so scared of being caught writing to you."

Thus I attempted the obligatory lover's lie, since the night before I had slept quite well, my cat against my cheek, and my parents had no suspicions. Besides the great love she believed she had in her heart, she had nothing, or so little to say, that seventeen-year-old girl, who crept furtively to the station to drop her letter in the mailbox. She did not yet know how to cover page after page, stretch it out, laboriously improvise the chronicle of a village where nothing happened.

I hope the recipient had the good taste not to keep those young letters, dressed in their Sunday best of thick and thin strokes, and an industrious handwriting, because I had retained a child's writing for a long time, large and awkward, and it was just beginning to make me blush. Out of zeal and coquetry I bought a copy of *Graphology* by Crépieux-Jamin. But adolescence quickly grows tired of cold dissections. I stopped trying to question certain *t*s, certain *f*s with lines curved like a potbellied ant. I gave up hope of endowing my writing with signs that clearly disclosed my loyalty and diplomacy, artistic talent, and intemperate sensuality.

But more of a handwriting analyst than I imagined, I eventually trusted to my vague and violent instincts, in the divinatory difficulties that an unknown writing inflicts on me. There are many of us who scrutinize a closed envelope in the same way: first the address, turn it over, turn it over again, then the letter, sniffed, inspected, finally read. At the bottom of the message the last surprise awaits us: the signature. Pay close attention! This is where the man reveals himself with his panache, the woman with her guile, the serpent with the whack of his tail like the flick of a whip, the insane person with his floral calligraphy, the fool with his little frizzy spirals, the eccentric with his thick period that he places absurdly in an interlaced design. And if the falsely energetic inscribes there his short flourish ending in a blotch, we also have the falsely modest, who proudly suppresses all flourishes. That's where the secret portrait is hidden.

I didn't love my laborious love letters. I only loved the responses, the other voice of the duet. I admired the man's fine writing, gladiate, obliquely ascendant, that shot out aggressively and nimbly. Of this eloquent arabesque, a work of the human hand, I envied the ease, the fiery and personal style that kept the writing so condensed that I often had to resort to a magnifying glass to decipher it. One of his traits should have worried me, a sort of agoraphobia that made his writing shy away from the page's open spaces. He made bizarre use of the margins, the angles of the page, the flaps that glued the envelopes shut. On these tiny triangles were massed microscopic writings, taking refuge far from the center, rising in tiers above the hypotenuse. I should have thought about this, or at least mused about it. We are strange creatures, at heart so uncurious about one another. The fine handwriting of a man riled me like a passionate image. The mysteries of his manner of expressing himself made me suspicious of the messages that love uses for its mission of translating a great disorder. "Just the thought that you will read these lines," writes the lover, "makes me tremble." "Why didn't you come to me?" writes his lover. "Tears blind me, I barely know what I'm writing." Meanwhile, imperturbable, in parallel lines, slanted and twinned, downstroke follows downstroke. My letters written out on the bench of the station say, "Hastily I scribble this to you. . . ." Hastily? I was taking great pains to write neatly every *l, j, h,* and nothing was rushing me.

But everything changes. Authentic sorrow and passion tussle well-set curls, shake the importance of the little even arcades of the letter *m,* and make for spelling mistakes. Old pages still quiver enough to make me remember again. A gnawed stub of red pencil, poorly sharpened, was enough to say everything. Does one ever have a pen in hand when the urgent moment arrives, when the minutes count? Quickly, on any old scrap of paper: "My love . . ." Two words, that feverishly took up the width of the page: "My love . . ."

If it wasn't that one, it was one like it, the brother of the dull red pencil, that I resorted to later, to write three other words that took up as much space; and had as much spirit, as much tender haste: "My darling daughter . . ."

Letter to My Daughter

Colette describes auctions to sell literary rights to benefit destitute writers. Her daughter, Colette de Jouvenel (known by her nickname Bel-Gazou) was her only child. Published in *Les Lettres françaises* on October 12, 1950.

I miss those "sales" where writers sold off their own products to benefit their colleagues. I attended reluctantly, but from the moment I crossed the threshold, I was engulfed in the warmth and the brutality of the sale, the direct exchange of a book for money, the real presence of money, paper money, silver money, money that, in the blink of an eye, we all knew, men and women alike, how to calculate (but subject to error); the greed of a moment, that rivalry, which for an hour, made us forget literary rivalries.

For me, age and malignant arthritis have changed all that. So, go ahead, my daughter, take my place among the fragrant colonnades of freshly printed paper, struck with black letters, and sell my books. I have a level head, it doesn't get swayed by pride or false modesty. Your role is to use your personal taste, young and bold. So sell my books anyway you like. I also know which ones are the best, and if I wanted to, I could cite several sentences to denounce them as a bit disloyal: weren't they more concerned than necessary with their effect on the reader?

Don't even hold back on putting up for sale the works of mine that you like the best. Show some favoritism toward little *Gigi*, fairly recent; *The Blue Lantern*. *Earthly Paradise*—this last-born, will it be my last? *Chéri*, slow to age. People still read *The Vagabond*, and my stories about animals. But don't think, even though it's less read, that *The Other One* is inferior to *Julie de Carneilhan* or to *Green Wheat*. It's just an attitude that certain of my novels take on. A little attitude—bless their hearts!—of true modesty, and it suits them rather well.

The Young Poet

A fine example of Colette's sharp irony, and her original and subtle take on the battle of the sexes. First published in the newspaper *Le Matin* on November 13, 1913.

The young poet writes to me often; he readily writes to women of letters, notable actresses, and benevolent and well-read women. It's not always the same "young poet," but he always "hesitates" to write to me, and he has tossed his verses "twenty times" into the fireplace, he is dying of the confusion caused by dedicating these to me, chiseled for me, inspired by me alone. Though he doesn't hesitate to describe the "shyness of a twenty-year-old poet," he will mention that he feels boiling up in him the "adventurous passion of youth"; but he will never fail to insist in closing on the "respect" that he bears for me.

I turn the page, or I unroll the sheets of lined notebook paper tied with a pink ribbon, and from the first verses, I am spoken to in the familiar *tu* form, apostrophized with the most intimate lyricism, invited to celebrations of the heart and of the flesh, and led toward paradises or hells that I don't care about in the least, hand in hand with a young man I've never seen!

If the "young poet" would dare to say to me, in simple prose or speaking to me in person, a quarter of what he rhymes, he would be rewarded immediately with a couple of good slaps. But what to do? Sonnets, rondeaus, and ballads—he only sends me verses. He has found the most serene, the most unpunishable form of insult.

Fashions

Colette meditates in this piece on gender role reversals. She begins by talking about fashions in the Roaring '20s, and then she takes a surprising turn and shows a parallel with the literature written in the wake of World War I and its terrible toll of casualties. It was around this time that women began shedding nightgowns and dresses in favor of the formerly masculine pajamas and pants. First published in *Le Matin* on December 8, 1923.

Women's fashions are masculine. Fashion would have us cut our hair, open our collars; it insists on pajamas, arms the little hand clothed in a fencing glove with a thick cane when she goes walking, and I'm not even going to mention the mad consumption of tobacco—cigarettes, cigars, and pipes—and alcohol. It's just a craze, they say, bad taste, feminism; they also denounce the unpardonable freedom of young girls, and the substitution, demanded by the hecatomb, of women for men in all professions, white collar or blue. Meanwhile, man, tightly strapped, pumiced, wears a corset belt and silk underwear. I don't see any danger, social or moral, in such a reversal. In their hearts, the women of our countries did not wait for the war to accept the luxuries of men, and sometimes men as a luxury. But in any case, times have changed, and women are anxious. A rarer prey, of a finer quality, escapes her right now. Failure, flight, redouble women's covetousness, and lead her inevitably into a frenzy where passion never fails to imitate what it cherishes most. So women tie cowboy bandanas around their necks, wear wool trousers, and sprint the hundred meters. You see her, flat as an Annamese, panting under the custard of rugby fields, naked and oiled to swim across a river, and you call a battle of the sexes what is only devotion—the feminine paying homage at the feet of the masculine.

I see a similar trend toward "inflation" in novels.

For a literary series, I handle in one month about fifty manuscripts. Only twenty years ago, there would have been an abundance of feminine work with an autobiographical slant. At that time, these "studies of a young girl" endowed literature with demonic adolescent girls, mischievous gamines. In dubious detail, the author surveyed this ungrateful age, the marriage or emancipation of the heroine, her first fall—today such tales are about as exciting as a dethroned boxing champ.

Now it's Narcissus who confides in us through the narrative, expressed in some two hundred and fifty pages or more, of his early childhood, his first communion, the anxiety of his teenage years. An amazing seriousness emanates from these new novels and guides a few of them toward glory.

The scrupulous, the loud, and useless veracity of these narratives, sometimes lead to results that are humorous—but not for long. The rest of us—women who also scratch on paper, rivals whom the infatuated public are turning away from, forced to complain privately to ourselves, and to resort to an artificial simplicity—faced with masculine subtlety—we are the first to understand the hidden meaning of the sweet verbiage that escapes the young male writer: "Lean on me, on everything that comes from me. And stay serious. There is nothing of me that is not important, woman, since the war has made of me a living commodity without a price, from now on greedy for itself, penetrated, fragile—because I'm a man."

Why I've Never Written a Children's Book

Way ahead of her time, Colette was an ardent believer in the sophistication of children. She never portrayed them as guileless innocents in her fiction, and in her essays she defended their right to be treated as full human beings in their choice of reading materials. First published in *Marie Claire* on December 31, 1933.

Every year when people are giving books as holiday presents, they press me to write a children's book. Readers trust me, and they assure me that I would succeed at it. But I don't dare. It's too difficult. The respect that I have for children holds me back any time I try to start a novel for them.

In my distant childhood, there was literature for "youth." As soon as I set my eight-year-old or ten-year-old eyes on one of those books, I felt disrespected. A good number of those books are still sold, by which I mean, you still find them *being* sold. A few of them cross the thresholds of schools, imposed on thousands of students.

I will not restrain myself from naming, in order to stain its reputation, *Two Young People from Alsace-Lorraine Tour France*, if I'm not mistaken. I still remember its sugary morals, and its mercantile sentiments.

The very idea of writing a novel, a short story, a fairytale, makes me hesitate. Where, for a child of today, is there a fairyland? Children never stop fooling us, fooling themselves. The little boy who cares only about airplanes, the radio, and cars, and who imagines himself as a future pioneer of industry or as a gangster—one and the same for him—caresses in secret a dream he doesn't reveal; and a hope that the sky, now accessible, leads to a place that only grace or magic can open. What could I give him? I'm afraid of boring him if I try to appeal to his artificial precociousness, and if I address his hidden romanticism, he would turn away from my book in embarrassment.

I'm also suspicious of the little girl and her hardness. What a severe judge! Before puberty softens and intimidates her, her judgment spares nothing. She has a sharp sense of irony, an angelic insensitivity, which, in contrast to boys, she clothes in sweetness. How many times does she imitate femininity, which suits her? Who knows what she really loves? For recreational reading, doesn't she only value forbidden books? She exclaims—I've heard her—while rejecting with one gesture a popular series of books: "Oh, no! Nothing with that cover!" Illustrations don't work any better: "Why do they always give me books where everyone wears fashions from two years ago? Just look that those skirts!"

Someone once said, "Children's books should be written by children." That's truly a grown-up's idea—actually, the idea of a grown-up who doesn't have any children. It wasn't long ago that we were confounded by samples of literature written by children. Collected into one volume, I would not suggest it as reading material for any mother. Affected, plagiaristic, with fake naïveté—ugh! Those under twelve fill us with fear. Whose fault is it? Let's not whip ourselves, let's just put a stop to the publicity that lauds, in tears and superlatives, these prodigies under age ten. What? Silence a budding writer? But of course. I only see it as positive. Martyrdom does to a true calling what a good rainstorm does for peas.

I'm not fond of ending with unilateral advice. To advise our children not to write too early is good, to write so they read would be even better. But I'm not going to comply when I have the feeling that we adults often get mixed up in what is not always our business.

Our role is often tactfully to ignore, to collect from the space behind the bed, in silence, the forbidden book, or not to violate brutally the secrets of a desk. Let's imitate at times the delicate discretion of a fourteen-year-old boy, who was able not to tell his family about the explosive scandal that was resounding through his school. When his mother criticized him for not informing her about it, he responded, embarrassed, turning his head away, "Stories like that aren't for parents' ears."

Children's Books

This surprising and uncompromising view of children's literature reflects Colette's thoughts on how young people are often condescended to and underestimated. *Monsieur Tringle* is a whimsical chapter book for children written by Champfleury (1821–1889) and first published in 1866, in which a rich bachelor dresses up as a devil to woo an even richer girl. Charles Perrault (1628–1703) is the most famous teller of fairytales in French, similar to the brothers Grimm in German. Walter Crane (1845–1915) was an English illustrator of children's books in the Victorian era. Madame de Ségur (1799–1874) was a widely read children's author. Marie-Madeleine Franc-Nohain (1879–1942) was a popular illustrator of French baby books and picture books. Colette's article was first published in *Le Matin* on January 22, 1914.

As one of my young nieces said with a discouraged look as she flipped through a holiday gift book, "Oh, no! It's enough to make you disgusted to be a kid."

I asked her to explain, and she added, "You know what I mean! It's complicated to explain. All the books they give us, they reek of grown-ups, grown-ups who want to put themselves at our level, to make themselves younger, who purposely try to be simple and not to use big words. Well, it's too obvious, and it's humiliating to me. Do I go around writing books for grown-ups?"

I didn't say anything, and my niece, encouraged, continued: "Look, most children's books have the same effect on me as people who come to visit who don't have kids and know nothing about us, the ones who always ask me, 'So, my little friend, are we working hard in school? What year are we in?' I don't know if you remember your childhood, but those people make me want to answer with the ugliest words I know—and I know some really ugly ones."

I imposed silence, in the name of good upbringing, on my sarcastic niece, and I foolishly told her that my childhood was too distant, and that I'd almost forgotten it.

But in fact I have forgotten almost nothing of that faraway time. I remember that with the exception of several striking picture books by Walter Crane and *Monsieur Tringle*, I possessed few children's books, because I didn't like them. I was only interested in the ones I just mentioned for their formal beauty, but the text of books devoted to youth hardly interested me at all, and even the sadism of Madame de Ségur, that "pink library"—where they flagellate, where they roll around in tantrums, where they cut up living animals—did not retain my interest.

It seemed to me then—it still seems to me—that children, aside from the classic volumes intended to instruct them, can do very well without the novels written for their consumption. It's a useless task to reduce and to organize feelings and actions down to size when grown-ups judge them to be, in their eyes, excessive. Excessive! What can we teach about heroism, about tenderness, about sorrow, or even about love to shy children, who carry them inside and hide them, even to the point of sometimes making their swelling hearts and too-small bodies burst? Their emotional subtlety, we are meanwhile warned, humbles and disconcerts our own; what then are we sparing children, in coming up with novels for them? Difficult words? They don't fear them—on the contrary. If a child is bright, eager, and precise, he will be able to question and translate; if not he will cherish for a certain time the mystery, the music, and the variegated lights of the beautiful "word that he doesn't understand."

For as long as the novel has existed, all parents in the world have happened upon, in a corner of the library, a schoolgirl with hot ears, made wild by a forbidden book, which is confiscated from her with these words: "What can you possibly understand of this? It's not appropriate for your age!" while the adolescent who is chastised has given up play and sleep in honor of the delectable book: I could tell you the name of someone who was once a young girl, who read daring stories in the light, a thousand times extinguished and relit, of a thousand wicks. An adolescent would sulk or blush if she was accused of seeking, in her clandestine readings, what preoccupies the unhealthy imaginations of grown-ups, but she would rarely deign to justify herself, to explain herself, to escape one moment of her minimized look of a child, and to reveal, before her puerile mother and her forgetful father, the secrets of a soul that has no age, and a heart that is already ripe.

The ingeniousness of writers who devote themselves to childhood welcomes, at its best, that of painters and modern illustrators, and their work creates our joy, for those of us who see in a book, only a book. The child we give it to—after we have browsed and even read it for our own pleasure—the child is more circumspect, does not bond with it right away; he discovers, and when the need arises, he invents, complicated seductions that transform his book into a fetish, a companion for walks and snacks, a refuge against sorrow and boredom. The former reasons don't depend entirely on the text—far from it—nor on the pictures. I call on my memories of being an ordinary little girl, neither nervous, nor sickly, nor a prodigy, and I can list my literary preferences of those days: a blue book, illustrated in the margins with birds and flowers, never left my room, and I only had to open it, to whatever page, to taste a bizarre pleasure in the design of the petals of its roses, carefully curled up like a snail. The title, the words of the blue book? I've forgotten. I liked another volume because of the mischievous shape of the lowercase *a*, which had a little hook on its rear. And if I opened ten times a week the adventures of *Monsieur Tringle*, it wasn't to laugh at his all-too-well-known tribulations, nor at the "street urchins who, drunk on joy, ran through the streets shouting, 'Fire!'" but because I knew that on a certain page a winter moon brightened a sleepy, thatched cottage, a moon so bright and blue, glacial, implacable, that I played I was shivering when I contemplated it. I have in front of me the most charming, the most successfully realized picture book. At the top of its white leaves, narrow borders seem to open the pages halfway onto a baby's nursery; just enough room for the round head of a newborn, the fine chin of a disheveled young mother, an awkward little naked foot, a tiny hand in a wool glove, a brown lock of hair, eyelashes lowered to a dimpled cheek, a nurse's hat, a bassinet, a branch in bloom hanging from an invisible tree. The beginning of a life is depicted there with calm art and love, everything teaches you that maternity is neither an overwhelming miracle nor an abnormal state of anxiety. And the engravings are made to be small, leaving a great deal of room for the "Baby's Journal," for the baby's footprint and handprint, for dates, for memories where the infant is front and center. But this, Madame Marie-Madeleine Franc-Nohain, is not a book *for* children, it is, thank God, a *baby* book, for grown-ups.

A book "for youth" is a perilous undertaking of men and women who have forgotten their own. How many have failed at it, since Perrault—whom I don't even know. I didn't want to read you, "immortal tales of Perrault," because Gustave Doré slid, between your pages, a black castle pierced by glowing windows; a cat standing bolt upright in his crenellated boots; a princess on her carriage, dreaming and turning toward me her face and her arm as white as the gigantic sickle moon. I didn't read you, because when I read you my exaltation was deflated, and I quickly flew back to the haunted castle, to the fugitive princess, and even to the cover of this large book, with its ripples of little waves, like a spring, also wonderful, where the Dragon slept. Then I left behind all these fairies, and secretly I attacked another brick in the enormous Balzac, the way a puppy gnaws, with his brand new teeth, the foot of a massive door.

Scribes of the Palais-Royal

Colette lived the last decades of her life in an apartment in the Palais-Royal, a famous building located in the center of Paris. As its name indicates, the Palais-Royal was once the palace of the kings and queens of France, before the Louvre was built. Later, the Palais-Royal was subdivided into stores and apartments, and many writers lived there. In French the title of this piece is a play on words, since it means, "Scribes of the Royal Palace." First published in *Gutenberg informations* in January 1939, issues 2 and 3.

Everyone talks about what he knows. One about his sadness, to calm or treasure it, another about his love—same thing there—others about their work, or about the narrow universe within their field of vision. This generous and naïve inclination, which leads us to free the truth in ourselves, is the perpetual temptation of the writer, just as that of the painter is to paint what only he sees.

But once the lamp is lit and the curtains are drawn, with resignation, I have to invent. There is no point in appealing to fever, which refuses to be the climate of the prose writer. Our sources are based on methodically distorting the truth.

In forty years of work, I've had the time to compare, from the point of view of how much they do or do not assist me, the sites where I work. I am not at all one of those privileged persons who plant their table right in the middle of a patio, delight in an alp or a lake, welcome a few rays, a butterfly, wind, and birds. As for the perpetual moral discomfort that the duty to write represents in my life, for a long time I've associated it with physical discomfort—the armchair too low to the ground, the wobbly table, a lamp I came across by chance. But maturity, and then old age, teaches us—thank God—that we can have both demands and choices. By choice I have come, and come back to the Palais-Royal. Are there, in this rectangular cloister haunted by pigeons and cats, any idle people? I don't believe so. I suppose I might find it melancholy, this sequestered garden, if I had long hours of leisure. The "square" of the Palais-Royal is not a retirement home: the somewhat slapdash arrangement of its spaces, its skewed partitions, its parquet floors like Russian mountains, all of which, behind its beautiful and rigid façades, ages, plays, crumbles, and changes—it seems to attract active guests. Closest to the Louvre reigns Georges Huisman and his hive. The long Montpensier Gallery shelters Paul Reboux, Emmanuel Berl, Mireille. The *Paris-Soir* newspaper delegates to us Pierre Lazareff, Hervé Mille, and Maurice Goudeket; and Ribardière, who represents *L'Intransigeant*. The setting sun illuminates the charming face of Marcelle Vioux, bohemian Eve framed by all the animals of her Earthly Paradise. Facing south, the Beaujolais Gallery houses me. That's where I drink in the sunlight, and on clear nights the moon goes hunting outside my windows.

How silent we are! Our regular nighttime vigils make less noise than the dance of dry leaves in the enclosed garden, less noise than the claws of the tomcats carding the tree bark. By daylight, my thick lodgings—the Beaujolais Gallery puts twenty yards of masonry between the street and the garden—is hardly sonorous. But I'm lucky that a muffled vibration, marvelously identical to that of a propeller, gently rocks me. It's Robert Baze, the master printer, who feeds, on the ground floor, his presses. The huge heart of an ocean liner beats, spreads out with a dampened sound, counterpoints my own heart, embroiders and sustains a snippet of a song that haunts me. My sentence finished, the page filled, I embark, and on this anchored boat, I voyage.

On Growing Older

Colette wrote this essay in 1951, toward the end of her life. It was published nine days after her death in *Lettres françaises* on August 12, 1954.

I have been writing for more than fifty-three years now, and for more than fifty-three years the material worries of life—or fixed deadlines—have set the rhythm of my work and my existence. I promised my editor . . . My novel has to be done by November at the latest—novel, novella, a fictionalized anecdote—a fairly skillful blend, by the way, of fiction and reality.

I managed, all the same, but now my inability to walk and the accumulated years have put me in a position where I can no longer sin by lying, and they banish all possibility of romantic encounters. From now on I possess only what unfolds on the screen of my window; only lightning, from the heavens or from an eye; just the constellations; and the wonders that expand under my magnifying glass. So it is by the grace of God that I accumulate leaves of books, deprived as they are of distorted and likeable traits, of dialogues between imaginary people, of arbitrary endings—who slays, who marries, who separates. I abdicate my impostorings, but they will perhaps not be published, or even finished.

The hour has come for me to give myself over to reveries that are more vain, to the mental exercise that I must make do with till my end, and please note: my horoscope threatens me with longevity.

This damned broken leg, the origin of my arthritis, has compromised all my projects. Before that, I was counting on growing old the way my family's bay mare grew old. She was aged, tired, determined, and we used to say about her, "Next winter, we'll retire her. She's really earned it." But then winter began, and the bay mare was still hitched to the carriage. Winter finished, and just from hearing the shrill trumpet of the mare in her stable, we knew that the return of the good weather would see her once again out on the roads, climbing hills with a nimble gait, stopping to nibble the new shoots with her worn teeth. What can you do? She didn't like to rest.

I would not have needed as much persuasion as she did to accept my rest and my meadow, since I've always loved—with unrequited love—rest, and even laziness, but I would gladly have stayed hitched to my carriage for a longer time, still agile and retaining a taste for the road.

An accident and its consequences have defined my lot in life. I'm not complaining that it consists in the pleasure of staying home, while that of young people and those who are intact is to go out, but my lot requires only resignation—and that is actually the most difficult thing—as well as a healthy relationship between past and present.

At a quarter to seventy-nine, one still has projects, and I don't lack for them. One of mine is to live a little longer, to continue to suffer in an honorable manner, that is to say without outbursts or bitterness, and to laugh when I have cause, to love those who love me, to put in order what I will leave behind me, from my bank balance to the drawer with the old photographs, as well as my few pieces of clothing and a few letters.

To be true, to be ready, to set things in order—it's all one and the same.

Georges Wague, my former companion on the pantomime circuit, called me up: "What time is it?" Well, it's time to be summoned, just to be, in your bathrobe or woolen pajamas, to be clothed, in a clean shirt, with feet that are clean, and all the rest, too. It's a long road, my life, and my heart is long in experience. My instinctual inclination, which delights in the curve and the circle, contents itself superstitiously in those things. To reach toward the finish is to return to one's point of departure; the true adventurers don't go back there. But I won't hide from you much longer that I have nothing in common with actual adventurers.

No matter—I've always had fun along the way.

Colette's Journalism

Tinkerers

In this prophetic article written in the mid-1930s, Colette takes on the hot-button issue of foreign workers. She approaches this topic gently and with humor, through the subject of tinkering or handiwork, a favorite pastime of the French. By showing how much the international employees of the hotel where she lives are also consumed by this activity, she points out the common humanity between the French and the blue collar workers in a service industry. The phrase "my double, my brother" [mon semblable, mon frère] is from the end of Charles Baudelaire's great poem, "To the Reader." In Paris the water is high in minerals that leave chalky tartar or scales on kettles. The original date and place of publication of Colette's article are unknown, but estimated to be 1934 or 1935. Reprinted in *Cahiers Colette*, No. 2, 1980.

For the traveler who stops, leaves, and stops again, a hotel is just a way station with shadows—some helpful, some not—and always with their hands out. But at this hotel I'm the traveler who has stopped here for four years. Do you think it takes less time than that in a lodging of this sort for phantoms in tail coats, with mute soles, to emerge from the anonymity to which the passerby relegates them? They have the decency to remain invisible. It takes more than one vague and kind word to get them to come out of the walls. And you travelers, my brother nomads, you do not lavish your kind words on them. You are usually in the self-defense mode.

Not to mention that the room service waiter—carrying like a bullfighter with his cape, a table with its settings on one shoulder, or balancing on the extended fingers of a single hand the tray, the ice water, the whiskey, and the glasses—only reveals in his face, his most Swiss, Luxembourgian, or most banal Italian expression. And you grumble in your best French xenophobic voice: "Those foreign workers!"

Do you actually think, my double, my brother, that for one look a living creature will leap out of her milieu, throw a password at you, and be delighted to be recognized by you? It takes time, I'm telling you, the time for you to deserve an expression of pure sympathy. When this moment arrives, the clouds part, the desert becomes populated, human faces rush forward.

"Is this about tipping?" You are quite disillusioned—and for good reason—you always look for the worst motive, the simplest.

Place a little more trust in the improbable. Tell yourself that this might be a mask, this surface layer of a pink native of Freiburg shining with the cheeks of a sylph in a threadbare suit. And that Swiss man, acting more Swiss than is natural—has it ever occurred to you that he is camouflaged as a Swiss person? Scratch those sour façades a little: beyond his anonymity, which weighs him down, relegated to those whom you call "foreigners" and "stateless people," you will see arising a Frenchman as average as you or I, jack of all trades, presumptuous, but devoid of ambition—and a tinkerer.

Use has consecrated this word since it defines a trait in the French national character: we tinker with our hands. A charming little newspaper about animal husbandry and care, which provides some of my favorite reading material, offers work for "hired hands." In times past, more elegantly, they said: "a man who is good with his hands." One of my friends, an extraordinary handyman, says of himself: "I would only really be useful on a desert island."

In that exalted domain of indiscretion called tinkering, I boast that I can recognize a compatriot. But even if I don't sniff him out in advance, I'm delighted when his calling for handiwork is revealed to me.

From the little room where I write I can see—if I open it on all sides to every air current, as I had to do in the scorching week that just passed—I can see a corridor, and beyond that, a large landing. It's on this landing that a group of employees of the hotel were gathered, attentive to something lying there that I couldn't quite make out.

Leaning over, absolutely still like certain lepidopteron that are difficult to approach, were the ubiquitous room service waiter, and the winged bellboy who distributes the mail. The maid, a blue dragonfly in her gingham uniform, was also staring at a strong young man with a long mustache seated on the ground in the center of the group, with a ruddy complexion like a Burgundian. He works here as a carpenter and was making little precautionary taps with a hammer, and since my curiosity was piqued, I watched more closely.

I was astonished to realize that all that collective attention was concentrated on an object that seemed to me in itself unworthy—a flat sandal of thick leather, one of those Saint-Tropez sandals that I wear ever since an unfortunate incident when I broke a bone.

"You can hammer all you like," declared the waiter ironically as he flitted about. "What it really needs is some eights."

The vermillion carpenter stopped working at his makeshift repair. "Eights? What eights? These nails are the only thing for the job."

"Gotta have eights, and square," he insisted, in his best French accent, this waiter who usually speaks English. "My grandpa in Savoy, he made wooden clogs. I think I know a little about this! In work and cuisine, Savoy is number one. If I was you, I'd be using a wooden shoe nail. What's so funny, Marguerite?"

The blue dragonfly, fragile and petite, objected: "First of all, I'm not laughing, I'm coughing. And besides, I think that's ugly, that fat sandal. Where I come from, we don't like them. We're light-footed down there."

"And where is 'down there'?"

"Basque country. Nothing's as good as a sole made of rope. Now, we mountain people . . ."

"Oh no, there she goes again," cried the mail dispatcher, "with her little village, and her espadrilles and her fandangos. Let me tell you, for a tool like that sandal, I'd say to Madame Colette, 'If you're really looking for walking shoes, when it comes to serious walking, I know what I'm talking about, and I'd recommend . . .' "

"Enough with your serious walking!" interrupted the carpenter, offended. "Sell it somewhere else!"

"Monsieur Cauchois, I can hear you all the way in the linen room," a discreet voice reproached.

Mademoiselle Francine, the hotel linen maid, padded in on quiet feet, but without abandoning her favorite duties. A greasy rag and screwdriver in hand, she oiled and held up to the light an enormous revolver, which she showed off with pride. "It belongs to the gentleman in 603," she said. "I was changing the tulle curtains when I saw this revolver. 'Oh, monsieur,' says I, 'such a beautiful weapon, what a shame it's so neglected!' I'm cleaning the whole thing for him: tonight he won't even recognize it. Firearms and locks, now that's my kind of work."

The ringing of my telephone prevented me from learning more, and I left my listening post. But my loyal Pauline had already answered and hung up the phone.

"It's nothing," she said competently. "Somebody else who mixed up the Grasset edition of the *Complete Works* with the Flammarion limited edition! If it wasn't for me . . ."

She returned to her washing, and I closed the door behind her, since "my kind of work" requires solitude. By my kind of work, naturally I mean removing the scales from a copper kettle; and also the dismantling, repairing, refilling, and reassembling—all operations that, without stretching the truth, I can say that I excel at—of a lovely kaleidoscope from the Second Empire.

The Discovery

This piece concerns anesthesia for childbirth, which began in the mid-nineteenth century, but did not become widely available in France for several decades. First published in *Le Matin* on July 30, 1914.

"You will no longer give birth in pain. . . . You will no longer feel increase, hour by hour, the suffering that heightens with every contraction, to its fullest extent, to perfection—you know what I mean!—and then the next contraction adds another layer of torture. . . . You won't fill the air with persistent, rhythmic cries that sap your energy: in conclusion, you will labor in peace, in the silence that you deserve."

I muse for a long time on this discovery, the great discovery of Doctor Paulin. Theories about white sheets, where there are no moans. . . . Faces dazzled by having given birth almost in a dream. . . . Newborns brought by fairies, a serene era of miracles, though somewhat lethargic ones. . . . You have to marvel at, and everywhere trumpet this wonder: but who can I trumpet it to if not the woman with her heavy belly who is treading the path right under my window?

I don't know how old she is. I've always heard her called just Mother Sarcus. She is carrying her twenty-second child. The previous ones . . .

"How many living children do you have, Mother Sarcus?"

When she is asked that question, her thick eyebrows contract over large black eyes, still lovely: "Seventeen . . . hold on, what am I talkin' about? Sixteen, not more, 'cause of the daughter I lost last year."

She says "the daughter," and not "my daughter." She has been a mother almost as often, but not better, than a fertile cat, who forgets the kittens from her next-to-last litter. The child she just popped out she promptly gives over to the capricious care of an "older" girl of seven or eight. She willingly admits, speaking of her progeny: "Yeah, I forget their names," and she has ingeniously numbered them to keep track.

"Hey, Eighteen!" she yells, "as sure as there's a God, you're gonna get yourself a spanking! And you, Fourteen, I see you dawdlin' over there. Isn't it time for your school? When I tell you—yes, you, Nine—to find your father and get him to pull up the turnips, it's not so you can stand there teasin' your sister Thirteen!"

A chronic and great fatigue lulls her pride in these twenty-two births. She only boasts of delivering on time, and that "everythin's all wrapped up by early morning," so she can do her laundry at the fountain.

"Mother Sarcus, tell me something!"

She turns around and walks back slowly to rest her elbows on my windowsill.

"I'm just moseying down to pick some peas," she answers.

"You've got time. Listen, there's a doctor in Paris who's just found a way that women don't have to suffer in childbirth. That should interest you, shouldn't it? What luck, huh?"

"Well, isn't that something," remarks Mother Sarcus politely.

"Fantastic, isn't it?"

"Oh, definitely."

"Little Twenty-two you're carrying in there, wouldn't you be happy to bring him into the world just like that! Like a soap bubble. I remember hearing you scream all the way from here last year!"

"Oh, yeah, not many people slept that night. The midwife even said to me, 'A little moderation, please now, Mother Sarcus. If I were you, I'd stop right there.' And then, well . . ."

She lowers her eyes with a fatalistic glance at her inexhaustible belly.

"Listen, Mother Sarcus, I'll get the information in Paris, and if it's at all possible, I'll offer you, for your Twenty-two, a delivery without pain!"

Her face shuts down, she picks up her basket.

"You're not interested?"

She chews on a sorrel leaf and dreams as if grazing.

"It's not like I'm against it."

"There's no danger, you realize? No more screaming, no more pain. . . . A baby that arrives like magic!"

"Yeah, but."

"But what?"

She spits out her sorrel leaf to the side and says this odd thing: "So, where's the glory?"

Poverty Exists Everywhere

Another prophetic piece of writing, this one on homelessness. Thomas Virelocque was a popular caricature of an old tramp created by the nineteenth-century engraver Paul Gavarni (1804–1866) whose artwork sometimes documented the poor of his time. Colette's article was first published in *Le Matin* on October 30, 1914.

There's poverty everywhere—and beggars, too. A beggar and a poor person, they're not always the same. But in these times, how can you refuse a ten-centime coin, even to a "bad" poor person? One of my friends sometimes objects: "Oh, not that one! He smells of wine. And he looks like a spy." Then she turns around and starts running back: "What if I made a mistake? I'm going to give him two sous, but I don't trust him."

Yesterday, a very bad poor person parked himself in a deserted street in Passy. Wearing a jacket, with no visible shirt, his face hidden under a too-large hat, all I could see of him was a curved back, and two fine little hands of a scribe or a goldsmith. No eye contact, a mutter for a voice, and the threatening insistence of the professional, to whom one does not so much give charity as pay him a sort of fearful insurance against break-ins and crime.

Another beggar came toward me, a magnificent and reassuring type of the other school, a tramp, a real one, adorned with seventy-five years of life, with curly white hair, and the rags of Thomas Virelocque. He excused himself for brushing against me, and mumbled distractedly, "A little something if you would, madame." A twenty sous coin in the palm of his hand seemed to jolt him awake, and he showed me, raising his holy centenarian head, the purplish-violet, dark, and golden sunburn that is painted only on the cheeks of those who sleep out of doors, in the summer sun, during the biting nights of autumn, and in the dawn wind.

"Terrific!" he cried. "Great timing. I was getting bored because when you walk around just to keep warm, it's boring. It so happens that yesterday no one gave me anything. I can understand a little, people have better things to do."

All his wrinkles coalesced into a laugh, and he added in good-naturedly, "My age group isn't being drafted. It's hunger that made me leave the woods."

"Which woods?"

"Viroflay," he answered in a word.

"But there must be shelters that . . ."

"Shelters?" He recoiled, became suspicious. "Oh, I'm not ashamed, you know, especially with twenty sous. Look, let me explain: tonight I'll spend up to ten sous to eat, I'll get a bed for five sous, and that still leaves me five sous—holy cow!—for tomorrow morning. May the good Lord bless you—or whatever you believe in."

The good and poor man walked away on his astonishing slip-pers shaped out of old pieces of green carpet, and shouldered his bag again, which let fall several raw chestnuts. He passed the bad poor person in the jacket, now calmly occupied with checking off in a notebook the numbers of elegant, shuttered residences. Each of the men carried the baggage of his era and of his employment: one the knapsack of chestnuts; the other the grimy notebook that rejoined in his pocket the Browning pistol.

Neighbors

A probing and ironic look at how domestic abuse and violence are often ignored or dismissed by those nearby who might be in a position to report it. First published in *La République*. Original date of publication unknown.

"After two weeks of not seeing Madame X leave her dwelling, the neighbors began to wonder. . . ." It takes neighbors quite a bit of time to start to wonder. Minimum of two weeks. The neighbor who wondered the most, the least shy, takes it upon himself to alert the concierge, or the other neighbors, or the authorities. The result unfolds according to established ritual: a body is found, two bodies, suicide, accident, murder. Depending on its mood, public opinion honors differently the touching discretion of the neighbor, who takes the secret to the grave—someone else's grave, of course.

This generic discretion is not the only peculiarity of the neighbor, who is also subject to an unpredictable sense of smell. We see him nervous and intolerant when he encounters a garbage can left out too long at the foot of the stairs.

Disapprovingly he sniffs the vapors of sautéed rabbit stewing on the floor below him. He perceives the stench of a kitchen sink— someone else's kitchen sink—and rises in indignation against it. On the other hand, he remains completely unaware, for weeks at a time, of the gas leaking freely from the apartment next door; and even of the strong, imperious odor of organic decomposition.

The neighbor suffers many sensorial aberrations. His gaze sometimes pierces walls, sometimes falters to the point where he can't tell the difference on a child's bruised cheeks among black and blue marks, scabs from burns, and muddy trails of tears. His sense of hearing, which allows him to count maliciously from behind the wall, the number of amorous effusions coming from his female neighbor, suddenly disappears when the sighs give way to sobs, even appeals for help, the piercing cries of a tortured child. But what the neighbor will not part with is his sense of dignity, which he holds high during interrogations, when he adds to the title of neighbor that of impartial witness.

"Did you know, Madame Neighbor, that the woman named Z. was torturing her child?"

"Well, I guess I suspected as much, Your Honor, like everyone else." [*sic*]

"And you never thought about intervening?"

"I couldn't, Your Honor, since she and I weren't on speaking terms."

Worse than formalities, the neighbor is also the victim of his own sensitivity:

"You weren't aware, Mister Neighbor, that your neighbors tied their baby to his bed and deprived him of nourishment?"

"Who me? It made us sick, my wife and me. After six months of it I finally said to my wife, 'If this goes on any longer, we're moving!' My nerves were shot and my stomach was all in a knot."

And that neighbor was telling the truth. We can believe, good neighbor that he was, that he lost his appetite and sleep; fled his lodging. No doubt he is the one who wrote an anonymous letter to the authorities to assuage his conscience and regain his nightly repose.

There's no question that relations among people are difficult. A wolf lies in ambush behind every door, ready to hurl himself on another wolf if he enters. Up until now, communism in our country has only happened outdoors and in meeting halls.

With us temperate Latins, the neighbor doesn't like others entering his home. He assigns certain kinds of effusiveness to certain enclosures: cafés are for fun, restaurants for face-to-face explanations, and he keeps domestic drama within four plaster walls.

Beyond these ideal limits, a cry occasionally escapes that is the equivalent of a border violation, of the horrific revelation at the opening of a mystery novel. Hearing it, a neighbor, a novice in her duties as a neighbor, turns pale, drops a plate, runs to throw herself into the mix and help.

Then the prudent hand of an experienced neighbor stops her, and turns on the radio.

The Fake Pearl

Colette apparently wrote this article in response to a scandal caused by the sale of a fraudulent pearl at a very high price. First published in *Le Matin*, October 30, 1913.

"Diamonds—yes, they're pretty, but pearls are . . . I don't know how to put it, but . . . well, you understand."

I've heard this sentence more than twenty times, left suspended in midair, and mysteriously finished off by the same gesture, a brushing together of the fingertips, as if rubbing an aromatic leaf or a pellet of balm, the gesture that the seller of gems uses at the moment when he caresses and seems to mould, in front of me, a round pearl.

"Three hundred thousand . . ." he sighs. "She's a beauty, isn't she? I'd like her for myself, but she's so high-priced!"

I wanted to gather some pointers on the affair of the fake pearls, but this lapidary at first only uttered disdainful monosyllables, the *pffs* of a superior man who does not let himself be "taken for a ride" by obvious frauds.

But even his reticence, his offended shoulder shrugging, reveal the part he plays in the scandal of the fake pearl. An inordinate scandal, from the outsider's point of view, since we just say, "Somebody faked a huge pearl. Big deal!" While the pearl-wearing aristocracy, the "true society," who wear pearls worth one hundred thousand francs to a million, are in a major uproar. A false pearl substituted for a real one, that was just a vulgar theft, harmless, promptly recognized, but a pearl that's "worked," a commoner without a pedigree, without a past; a glittery, doubtful, and fragile newcomer . . . Can't you feel rising against her, against her suspect sisters, the outraged rumor that greets the wife of a tax farmer-general, the first night she sits down next to a duchess?

The dealer in precious stones is still holding the round pearl, enormous, that he tenderly says he wants "all to himself." He plays with it, he tastes the never-to-be-imitated softness of this soapy "skin" that grates against your teeth if you bite it and warms so quickly in the palm of your hand. He holds it up against the light, satisfied with that line of creamy light that spills over the contours of that marvel, like the margin of brightness that outlines a star during an eclipse.

"She's a beauty," he says. "And fine all over, see? Perfect flesh and not a single flaw. She kills whatever comes near her. I'm having a little cushion made for her out of white batiste; she was bored on this satin—too mirrory. She is . . . she is . . ."

He searches in his professional vocabulary for higher praise, he holds up between two fingers the round ball, intact, not pierced, and pink as a breast under a white veil.

"She is," he says, "the color of love."

Gold

At the time Colette wrote this article, it was apparently illegal to sell gold in France, and there had recently been a high-profile arrest of gold traffickers. Bel-Gazou was Colette's daughter. First published in *Le Matin*, December 1, 1923.

Those who traffic in gold are, at present, ordinary businessmen, except for their honesty. Their forbidden commerce thrives in the shadows where it would be quite easy, no doubt, to reject this uncomfortable cloak, since it no longer adorns itself with an alchemical reflection, with the red glow of an infernal light, with the clinking of old doubloons, the pouring out, from a slit-open sack, of a pale stream of powdered gold. People buy and sell gold because there is always someone who will buy and sell what one must neither buy nor sell. But if it is currently illegal to exchange gold for another medium of exchange, the guilt goes farther back. The attraction of the yellow metal, the vocation of gold, emerged from the bowels of the earth at the same time as gold itself, and not silver, nor any other metal that is even more rare.

Do there exist, among greedy obsessives, among kleptomaniacs, people who are mad about platinum? I would be astonished. I would be less astonished to discover, in one of the gold traffickers arrested this week, in the well-hidden depths of his conscience as a dishonest man, at the heart of his first weakness, a savage and religious thirst for gold.

We all had, in former times in our families, that cardboard box, that little chest of arbor vitae burl where our mothers, our aunts kept remnants of gold: broken links of chains; worn-out rings; broach pins; the cotyledon of a medallion stripped of its matching half; antique and light circles that lost, when they broke, their cameos; the whole of it weighing three grams, five grams at most.

"It's gold—you don't get rid of it," said our mothers.

"So, Mama, what do you do with it?"

"You keep it."

"Why?"

"Because it's gold."

I remember when I was a child there was a little boy who wanted some of the louis and half-louis coins in his mother's change purse. They were found like those in a magpie nest, hidden, intact. The little boy—scolded, interrogated—wriggled foolishly.

"Tell me, Mimile, tell me why you took them, the yellow coins?"

He did actually answer the foolish grown-ups and surrendered to them the secret of his prodigious, ephemeral, mystifying senses.

"Because they smell good," he said.

Before him, crazy people, between two sessions of hydrotherapy, have spoken of the "perfume of gold." They proclaimed its voluptuousness and resemblance to human skin: one said it tasted like garlic, and licked a gold coin. But we don't lend credence to the hyperesthesia of the mad.

My old Persian cat, who died at an advanced age, experienced from a young age a powerful attraction to gold. I didn't discover it until the disappearance of a chain, a barrette, a pin—all gold—and a patient stake-out by the servant whom we had suspected.

"Madame, come look," he whispered one day.

Behind the glass door I spied the cat, magnificent in her blue angora coat, swerving into my room, her head up, sniffing the air. She leaped onto the writing desk, bit a pin, set it down. From the table she jumped to the fireplace, picked up from a dish the chain that was lost, found, and lost again. She wasn't playing when she made the little yellow serpent glitter with her bent paw. She seized it in her mouth, jumped down, passed through the door, and dropped the stolen goods at my feet when she saw me; but she didn't run away. She stayed there, embarrassed, not knowing what explanation to give. Twenty times later, I laughed when I surprised her in the process of making off with the same chain. Each time she abandoned it, perplexed, victim of a thwarted plan.

I would find the English pin again chewed up, bent, in the company of links of a gold chain, a watch bezel, a piece of a gold mechanical pencil—the same box that gnaws at the curiosity of my daughter.

"What's this for, Mama?"

"Nothing, Bel-Gazou. But I don't get rid of it."

"Why?"

"Because . . . because it's gold."

Laziness

In this personal essay Colette explores a neighborhood of Paris that is rarely tapped for its mystery, the formal area around the famous Avenue des Champs-Elysées. Despite the ceremonial aura of this wide thoroughfare, she finds much ambience in the side streets nearby. Sido was Colette's mother. The Bois de Boulogne is a park not far from the neighborhood of the Champs-Elysées. Charles de Rochefort (1879–1952) and Pierre Dux (1908–1990) were French actors of stage and screen. *Bajazet* is a tragedy by classic dramatist Jean Racine. Joseph Kessel (1898–1979) was a celebrated French journalist and novelist who wrote the book that the movie *Belle de Jour* was based on, and a famous song of the Resistance movement in World War II. Alexandre Stavisky (1886–1934) was a notorious financier and embezzler whose activities created a political crisis and scandal called the Stavisky Affair. The Cité Odiot is a U-shaped mews off the beaten path in this neighborhood that includes the former stables of the mansion of Jean-Baptiste-Claude Odiot (1763–1850), a famous silversmith who received commissions from Napoleon and Thomas Jefferson, among others. The fireworks at the end are from the Paris World Exposition, a world's fair that took place in 1937, which included Picasso's *Guernica* in the Spanish pavilion. This essay by Colette was first published in *Le Journal* on June 6, 1937.

Seasonally we see, with an accustomed eye, the return of June and of laziness. For those of us who are scratchers on paper, it's not until October that a sort of springtime rouses us, because July, August, garlic, and the South of France; the sea in Normandy and heavy cream; that precious diurnal sleep; and gymnastics not exclusively limited to one's right arm quivering on the page, all revive our appetites, including our appetite for work. But June gives dangerous advice. Too often I listen to the breeze from its youthful mouth, whose freshness Paris soon dries out.

Last week a Bastille Day July breeze wilted the flowerbeds, rolled the acacia blooms in a powder of dust; and from the little streams of the Bois de Boulogne rose the insipid dog days, and an odor of tench and dead frogs, which for me is the summons to inertia. It announces to me that an old horse, once more and for just a moment, is going to stop in its path. I will deal with him, since he is none other than myself. That is how Sido dealt with her mare Mustapha, who stopped dreamily and with her head hanging down in mid-course, oblivious to all scolding and even the whip. You had to wait until, deep in her dreams, the mare forgot her stubbornness, then you seized the moment, and with a light click of the tongue got her going again, without her realizing she was going again.

The conscientious writer is the person who tastes the deepest pleasure in turning away from duty. If the pleasures are filled with scruples, even better. If you drag them out, they pale. Then habit, by which I mean work, reclaims its rights. Who among us is capable, by practicing idleness, of rising to the wisdom that inspired this saying, worthy of a blessèd isle: Man is not made to work, and the proof is that it tires him out.

While dining in seventy-seven-degree weather, a crisis of laziness grabbed hold of me, the desire to escape from everything except a slow wandering that precluded choosing a route and a destination. What Paris neighborhood doesn't have its mysteries? The Faubourg-du-Roule and the Champs-Elysées are far from having lost theirs. Parallel to that great, multicolored, fairground of an avenue, the street where I dined reposes in silence.

Its name, now shortened, evokes princely stables, luxurious peace, the muffled shock of iron horseshoes against stall partitions. The vast garden of the S . . . mansion, opposite the little restaurant, overflowing with trees, birdsong, releases to those dining the scent of geraniums saturated by watering. Because of this scent, I knew that the detectives of the Capucines Theatre would be pursuing the murderer without me; that Charles de Rochefort himself could, without my seeing it, strangle in his fists the evil villain of a new play; and Pierre Dux was leaping in *The Versailles Impromptu*. As for *Bajazet* . . . There are June evenings when being irreverent about *Bajazet* is a need every bit as great as an ice cube tinkling against the sides of a glass of water.

The spectacle, the only one suitable for laziness, rises up right at our feet as soon as we begin to tread through Paris, between the day just exhausted and the morning that follows it. The stroller of the night believes he knows Paris because, freed from elbows and noise, he lifts his head and discovers the strange summits of houses, the only replaceable part where a citizen's imagination and thirst for escape can be satisfied. There he acquires a disdain for the middle floors, the preference I myself acquired, and believes only in inhabiting the deep ground floors, where the constant temperature of well-constructed cellars holds sway; unless a penthouse satiates his thirst for sunlight, downpours, and climbing rosebushes.

Leaving behind the shade, the heady linden trees, the long iron fence of the S . . . garden, I only wanted, followed by my straggler dog, to return home via the gardens of the Champs-

Elysées. But the gardens belong for six months of the year to the crowd, and I choose the streets that the night empties out for other purposes. Rue d'Artois, rue Frédéric-Bastiat, deserted, full of echoes—bars keeping vigil, garages that were once coach houses, coach houses that were once stables, courtyards equipped with watering troughs and wall fountains with huge copper spouts—so close to the avenue—what peace, only darkness. . . . The thick foundations of the houses secure, maintain the silence. At the very top are attempts at pergolas, balconies with added features, park benches, and bird cages, with the tough vegetation of Paris apartment buildings: bay laurels and balls of boxwood.

For Sale. For Rent. For Sale or Rent. The best is what remains empty, not yet devoured by the mania for construction that due to circumstances had to go unfulfilled. A blur of a cat, velvet on velvet . . . In the eight years I've lived in this neighborhood, a store has been having a continuous clearance sale at all hours of odd frivolities and perfume bottles, and I've never glimpsed a single soul in there.

Joseph Kessel springs out of a doorway, no hat, no vest, no tie. His shoulder bumps into a taxi as he crosses the street and disappears. Rue de Berri, an old mansion—the last luxury coveted by Stavisky—slumbers. Another mansion, at number 22, has its roof timbers gaping open, its shutters falling off, as if after an aerial bombing. Behind a hermetic façade beats a musical pulse, like a swarm of bees held captive. On the avenue itself and on the streets that cross it, beyond the humdrum apartment buildings, squat tiny "villas," each one adorned with its slender lilac bush, a chestnut tree, with a doily of grass spread in front of the door. A nightingale sings. . . .

On the rue Washington, as I pass the Cité Odiot, it sends out the yellow ray of its gas lamp to me, the bitterness of its trailing ivy, the sad cry of a nocturnal bird. A long life, oblivion, and happiness to the romantic Cité Odiot, unknown to so many Parisians! A hundred yards farther, the avenue, the neon lights, the orchestras, the restaurants find me the way car headlights pick out a hare dashing across the road. Eviscerated, drawn and quartered, the largest cafés gather two crowds; the crowd that's not drinking never tires of ogling the crowd that is drinking. A black pistil, standing in the middle of one of them, planted smack in the multitude, plays his violin. A Hindu family, seated on bundles of tied fabric, let the thin fingers of their brown hands hang down, and open the corollas of their eyes. A suave young black man who seems carefree presses a string instrument to his chest. Waifs full of grace, and perhaps sore at heart, these Orientals have been brought to our shores by the first convulsion of foreign curiosity.

Above the houses, toward the west, a pinkish fire drowns out the dusty constellations. From the top of a balcony, on the eighth floor, indifferent for one evening to all that is useful, meritorious, or simply professional, it's the time of day to watch in the sky the Exposition juggling several phosphorescent snakes, cocoons bursting into stars, and magic trees scattering their apples of fire.

With Love

This homage to the craft of French workers, particularly women, was first published in *Paris-Soir* on January 9, 1940, during the time when France was still fighting in World War II. The patriotic feelings, and the slighting of the German bride, can be seen in that historical context. So can the parcel being sent to the front at Christmas. Colette's views on work in this piece also reflect the ideas of the arts and crafts movement in England, with its emphasis on artisanship.

I watched the saleswoman assembling a parcel. As soon as I say "parcel," there's not a soul who will misunderstand me. The person sending the package, a wife or mother, had provided several items such as knitted woolens and foie gras pâté in a can. The candy store took charge of completing the shipment: mint pastilles and lemon-flavored ones for thirst, chocolate for hunger and sheer gluttony.

The saleswoman resembled many saleswomen in the week before Christmas, that is to say, having spent several days and nights on her feet, her hair was still neatly arranged, a bit dusty; her skin was dry; and as they say in the theater, the rouge was practically falling off her cheeks. But she did her work conscientiously, crammed the cans into the bottom of the box, padded the corners, and nested the sweets in the shredded paper.

It happened that the packets brought by the client, wrapped in a loud green paper, were in contact with those of the candy store, clothed in white with sky blue ribbon. So the saleswoman pouted her disapproval, untied the blue ribbon, and quickly replaced it with an orange ribbon. She did this of her own initiative, despite her fatigue, her unspeakable desire to sleep, her hurry, and her aching feet. She did it and made excuses almost at the same time as she opened up the loops of the ribbon:

"It's prettier this way," she says.

"You think?" says the client.

I would have paid a word of tribute to the saleswoman and her refined taste, but no doubt she did not expect any praise. She stands at the end of a long line of French artisans, whose personal taste still struggles with, intervenes in, emerges at every instant from anonymous manufacturing. A woman working on an assembly line is, with us, of sufficient quality; but in work her race triumphs above all when the French worker is able to judge, to control the work. I remember a quality controller of boxes of powder whose hand, in a vertiginous rhythm, sorted, saved, rejected the little cardboard drums. Without missing a beat, her eye caught the stains, the badly glued rim, the misshapen curve.

This critical temperament, which never leaves the French worker, doesn't prevent him from getting along with the machine, but he retains his individualistic view of it.

My saleswoman in the candy shop did nothing other than use her critical judgment, but the wonder is that she was able to display it at such a stressful moment, and in a way that was both extremely selfless and kind.

In this way she joins the ancient manual artists of the Far East who sculpted the soles of the feet of a statuette, chiseled the invisible underside of a doe's hoof and all the lines of the scales under the belly of a sea tortoise.

On my table, an old and lovely Chinese object represents three dates in chalcedony, and the hard stone imitates the half-dry, half-sticky epidermis of the date, with a perfection that does not admit of any lyricism. In a nook that the eye can barely penetrate, the sculptor of the chalcedony has reproduced a few sandy grains, scratches on the fine skin.

It's striking—striking and a bit banal. But with the orange ribbon, the anonymous saleswoman, and the unknown soldier—what a sentimental picture it makes, and how fluidly this anecdote guides us to a character trait! From the orange ribbon we immediately move to the fussy homemaker, who wants the wood floor under the bed to shine, and who matches, in the dark recesses of the armoire, the color of the perfumed sachet to the hanging on the walls.

Marcel Proust has immortalized the lining of Madame Swann's sleeves: a little hidden hem underlines the satin inside her jacket, a linen ruche embroidered in vain, doomed to remain incognito.

But the maid is worth all of Madame Swann and her refinements when suddenly she shouts; yanks the steel knitting needles out of the military sock that never leaves her; and undoes five rows, ten rows, twenty rows.

"What's the matter, Jeanne?"

"I started narrowing the rows too high up."

"No one would have noticed, since you don't even know who's getting the socks."

"Of course not. But it's sloppy."

Tiny stitches—six or eight to the centimeter in deluxe linge-rie—the end of the length of thread pushed back through the edge of the hem; the molding of the cornice, near the ceiling, carefully wiped; bias binding sewn to hide the stitches, a modest faux hem that masks limited resources at the foot of a skirt or a man's jacket, turned inside out, buttoned on the left; flowers on a table where there won't be a dessert; a cover in shiny colored paper used to dress up the old scuffed novel sent to a soldier; or the gesture of a high fashion designer of genius whom I saw one day, seizing hold of the prototype of a dress the way you shake a delinquent, turning it upside down, decking it out with flowers, brightening it up, so well and so quickly that we applauded—you are many testimonials to one and the same virtue.

A young German bride could not wrap her mind around the fact, thirty-something years ago, that her trousseau, sewn on a machine, inspired no admiration here. "But it's much more even," she said. And the rest of us, young women of that time, cried out, "That's just it!" For many years to come our hearts will hold a place for fine handiwork, fallible and intelligent, noble handmaid, capable of reworking patterns, capable also of follow-ing them proudly. A soldier on a break becomes an incomparable "arc-arator," that's what my native Puisaye called a handyman—to sculpt wood, draw, chisel a ring using improvised tools, provided he has the leisure to pour into what he does the quality of reverie, of solitude, and of invention that it requires.

Marie-la-Normande, who used to cook for my mother, one day opened the stove and received a shower of little embers on her linen apron that was then pocked with round sores.

The damage was irreparable, but she took it to heart that she had to fix it, and filled all the holes with needle lace, taking pleasure in proving that a cook was as good as a lace maker.

Marie-la-Normande also loved, as much as fine cooking, beautiful sentences, which she ornamented with her own reper-toire of phrases. For example, she predicted, seeing the clouds turning black, "I think the heavens are getting dark. Gonna rain out there, or who knows what'll come down."

The rose window apron, with as much openwork as a church, became an object of curiosity. My mother had Madame Pomié admire it and also Madame Légée, and they both burst out laughing:

"Your cook is crazy!"

"That apron is ruined!"

"She must have spent an awful lot of time on that! And it's exquisitely finished. Can you imagine! She put such meticulous work into it, such concentration, such . . ."

"No," said my mother Sido, "she put love into it."

The Silence of Small Children

This is an unusual tribute to infant children in the months before they learn speech, a surprising subject for a person of many words. The English nanny she mentions speaks French, but with many errors and malapropisms. The doctor who takes Colette to the childcare center, Clotilde Mulon, was an early and prominent French woman pediatrician. Paul and Virginie are the main characters in the novel *Paul et Virginie*, written by Jacques-Henri Bernardin de Saint-Pierre, published in 1787, and one of the seminal books of the Enlightenment, praising children's natural sense of justice. Colette's essay was first published in *Marie Claire* on March 31, 1939.

Everything concerning very small children puts me in a serious mood. Long ago, when I had a very pretty little girl—and don't think she's become ugly!—I was not one of those mad and delightful mothers who play with their babies, nibble them, laugh, double over with laughter, in short, I wasn't the type who seems to comprehend, among the bursts of happiness where aging is forgotten, that a brand new infant can get around without using its legs, express itself without words, communicate without sentences.

Almost always the spectacle of an infant astonishes me to the point where I am speechless. Before, I contemplated in my daughter the wonders that a creature of about ten months can produce, truly exalted, intoxicated with her daily discoveries, with the sound of her own voice, with her new ability to imitate barking or meowing, to repeat a snatch of a song, the chant of a laborer in the valley. The energy expended by a ten-month-old baby is incalculable. Our precious English nanny expressed so much pride in her:

"You go fights with her! Go ahead, shoot, look how strong his arms are!"

"I can't do everything," I answered. "I'm busy watching her."

Those early years, which our memories cannot reach, retain their mystery for us. We've forgotten the negotiating power of seven- to twenty-four-month-old babies, so their ruses confound us, their glares—heavy with dark rancor—intimidate us. At about seven months, the person I brought into the world developed a violent appetite for talcum powder, and, to our amazement, licked it through the holes in the container, which she seized while we were pinning her diaper after her bath.

"Hold his armses," said Miss Draper to me, "while I put on her little jacket."

A geyser of babbles came from the guilty party, immobilized on her back and extremely hopeful, despite the constraints. With her two free legs, she sought and found the powder container, grabbed it with her two naked feet that she raised up and brought up to her mouth with great agility. We don't always realize that our babies are born a little quadrumanous. But our impulse as adults, semi-paralyzed, immediately tend to take out of commission two hands out of four, then one out of two, depriving them of the left: "Zézette, don't let me see you eating soup with your left hand!" "Nono, your pencil! You do have a right hand, don't you?" And why not two, oh inconsistent parents?

Parents usually reserve this sort of advice for children who are quite grown and already a bit deformed, made in their image. My daydreams, my preferences are for the age when rapid growth multiplies the causes for astonishment, where the transformations that a child undergoes remind me of an iris opening, a large poppy that escapes wrinkled from its closed bud, or the butterfly's first moist hour. I love the fact that before their stammering and their first words, babies reduce us to divining, they push our intellects, take the "word" away from us. Later, they use the same means as we do to express themselves, charm, or lie: they are less interesting. For the nanny, who dedicates herself to taking care of the youngest children, there is often, besides her work, the thirst to dominate, the imperious curiosity about the dawn of the human. This older nanny was in the habit of saying, "I like them little, very little. At one day old, I take them. At one day old, there's already a person."

During the war I made friends with an admirable young woman whose friends have not forgotten her, Doctor Mulon. She gave all of her time and her strength, even to her death. She was the one who took me, knowing my penchant for contemplation, to Camouflage Childcare Center, way at the top of Paris.

"I've got some fine specimens for you there," she said to me.

There, in the beautiful light of Montmartre, babies who could not yet walk were playing on blankets. Clotilde Mulon introduced me to two little ones, nine and ten months old, sitting prettily and holding one another's hands.

"This is Paul and Virginie. What else could you call them? One mother brought Paul to me. Another set Virginie down next to Paul. They took one another's hand, stared at each other all day long, and at the moment when each mother came to reclaim her goods, we had two babies in the most unbelievably violent despair. But the next day—joy again! They're always the way you see them right now: they only play with one another, nurse well, but they only eat together, and as soon as they stop moving, they hold hands. I've never seen anything like it. But when you take care of children this young, everything is a marvel. Now come see another phenomenon."

The phenomenon, at first glance, looked like a blond doll with dark eyes, lost in knitted yellow overalls sized with the future in mind.

"She's ten months old today," said Doctor Mulon. "She was eight months when her mother first brought her here. The mother was desperately poor, but now works here at Camouflage. To console the little girl the first days she was here, we gave her toys, but she'd never seen a toy. So we put a doll next to her, but she'd never seen a doll. She looked at it terrified, without touching it. After three days, she picked up the doll, held it in her arms, and— listen to this! *She started to cradle it.* She cradled it so much that her whole little body, seated, followed the motion: she rocked to the left, rocked to the right. The appearance of the most maternal gesture at the age of eight months! I've seen a lot of things, but let me tell you! So, that kid, who invented motherhood, I named her Eve."

Colette on Her Life

Magic

In this article Colette claims that wizards and witches are very much alive in the countryside, based on recollections from her childhood. First published in *Le Matin* on November 10, 1923.

Black sorcerer, suggestion, fates, spells . . . another family bewitched, and if the daughter is crazy, chained, sequestered, it's the fault of a passerby, who caressed the father, mother, children with his evil look. All this goes on out in the fields, of course. Not that wizards and witches disdain cities, which provide a more reliable source of income. But this is all part of the romantic aura surrounding the wizard. A spell only works because of the conviction of the magician. The necromancer of the woods who suggested, in order to break a spell, that you throw into the flames the first person who walked by, was not at all motivated by humor, I would bet, or even cruelty, in muttering his macabre order. If you find him again, if he deigns to speak, you will see that he believes in his magic, so it follows that we also have to believe in the power of the "black wizard." Those who live or have lived for a long time in the country—the true, the sweet, impenetrable solitude punctuated by isolated farms, round ponds encircled by forests—know that magic, while its domain is shrinking, does not bow down before electricity, iron rails, and the telephone. A sibyl I know well will leave her sewing machine to sell you cabalistic advice; and an employee of the postal service will predict the future for you, will whisper to you the way to become invulnerable, to be loved, to protect against the evil eye. Many thaumaturges have become up-to-date. But the most rural, the most rich in peasant psychology have kept the medieval insignia of their craft, that is, the filth, the mop of hair untouched by the comb, the hut, the rags, the cane. Because they keep silent, a word that falls from their stingy lips can carry the full weight of someone's destiny. Dark, blending in with the uniform of the soil, they can move about unseen, but if you cross their paths, their omnipotence escapes from them, touches you in passing, and betrays who they are.

In my childhood I knew many a sorcerer. The handsomest was named Chickenbrush, a playful name that fit him like an earring on a tomcat. Old, silvery white, long-haired, his eyes shot out the black glance of a young man and looked at no one. Sometimes,

when autumn came, he hawked water chestnuts: "Prickly and tick-
ly chestnuts, chestnuts that tickle your thighs and prick your pockets!" Another, who only *seemed* to be meek, with little blue pupils
unfathomably deep, entered houses, and his little eyes compelled
you to buy contraband matches that lit all by themselves in the
corner of a sideboard. There was another whose evil spells I was
too young to know, but I revered him because he lived under a
public stairway and was known only by the name of "The Good
Lord." There were more. I remember that I found them sweet,
not at all scary, and that they decorated my village like gothic
gargoyles. But it's the same with sorcery as with love. One look,
one sigh in your direction may be harmless one day, but one step,
one prayer to heaven, and you're lost.

"Just a little bit farther . . ."

A meditation on a sort of negative luck, or more accurately, an absence of bad luck. First published in *La République* on December 17, 1933.

Do I have good luck? Don't doubt it, madame. First of all, I won sixty-six francs and sixty-six centimes in the National Lottery (there were three of us who went in on a ticket and won 200 francs). And then I once won, in 1908 or 1909, a thousand pesetas in Spain's Christmas lottery. Oops! I almost forgot a dozen coffee spoons made of "unalterable metal" that I once received in a raffle some artists organized.

That's it? Yes, that's it. I can see you're not impressed. But chance and I have had a different type of encounter as well. My kind of luck is not the jackpot or the windfall, the overwhelming one-of-a-kind fate that chooses you and bowls you over, exposed completely naked in front of everyone, riveted, forced laborer of the cocktail party circuit, picture on the front page of the newspaper between two brand new cars—one for weekdays, one for Sundays—and turns upside down the future of your children: "You were aiming for a garage, and the daughter of a corner store? The son of a millionaire is not for the daughter of a corner store! And you, Henriette, if I ever catch you yakking again with the herbalist's son!"

My kind of luck is luck without fireworks, a deaf confrontation with chance, a grain of sand from far away that makes my wheel skid, an orange peel, a tease that I neglect to avert, a sort of laugh of destiny that's just beyond my reach. My negative luck, I call "Just a little bit farther . . ." A little bit farther, and the chandelier in the living room would have fallen on my head—I felt, two centimeters away, the breeze of its fall, a strange vertical breath. I broke my leg two years ago. But just a bit farther for the car and me and that would have been the end for both of us, one underneath, the other on top. A little farther, one degree, two more degrees of fever, last winter during a lecture tour, and from then on I would only have spoken to shadows.

My life is already quite long enough for me to be able to recognize the features, balanced and reticent, of my luck by omission, almost by abstention, as opposed to positive luck. It doesn't advise me to extend my hand, to seize an opportunity, to adventure—just the opposite. We are not always of the same opinion, my luck and I. But if I don't hesitate to upset it, I am still fairly curious about what I would be without it, about the obscure woman I have left behind, and whom I sense getting older in a parallel life and in a place that doesn't exist in this world. A little bit farther, and she would have been the one taking my place.

"Watch out! A little bit farther and you would've stepped on a poisonous snake!" I still can hear my companion shouting this on a walk through the fields. During the war, my little house in Auteuil only caught a few shards during an air raid. "You know, madame, just a little bit farther and . . ." my old neighbor said to me.

Restraining hand, in charge of measuring the width of the abyss that separates "just a little bit farther" from "just a little bit nearer," I'm not asking you for explanations. But I would really like to know the name of the traveler, a good number of years ago, who got the last empty seat on a train that I wanted, that I *had* to take. Because of this occupant, I arrived "just a little bit" too late in a town where I had a booking. That's when it came right up to me, the car, readily available, of an unknown man, not to mention the unknown man himself. And the result of that encounter concerns no one but myself.

Movies, Theater, and Vaudeville

Why I Love Bette Davis

This is an excerpt of a longer article in which Colette discusses film actresses. *Jezebel*, a movie starring Bette Davis and Henry Fonda, was released in 1938, and features the famous scene where she wears a shockingly red dress to a party of Southern debutantes all in white. Valentine Tessier (1892–1991) was a French actress who appeared in many plays and movies, including *Madame Bovary, The Italian Straw Hat, Ménilmontant,* and *French Cancan.* This article was first published in *Marie Claire* on January 27, 1939.

I would like to have a reason why I prefer her to all the others, a reason less simple than my conviction that she is the greatest film actress. No doubt of the theater as well, when she is on stage. This tough granddaughter of Eve, overflowing with femininity, barely leaves other actresses next to her a chance to charm or to be noticed. See *Jezebel*: Bette Davis rules, drains the color from, and extinguishes everything around her, except the beauty of the landscapes, the animals, and the children—except what is, even more than she, close to nature, if not art.

In *Jezebel* Bette Davis enters the action like a gust of wind. Her first glance is enough to make doors slam, knock over flowerpots, and muss the hair of passersby. She mounts a large horse and handles its mouth roughly. In her hands, a fine mount would point like a dog. She drops the reins and throws herself into the respectful arms of a black servant, as if throwing herself off a bridge. I can find no other gesture so spontaneous, so burning except in Beaumarchais, when Cherubin springs out the window: "Into a flaming abyss: Suzon!" A comparison like that, even if fairly random, does honor to the American star.

From this sharply outlined apparition, to the final cart that carries the heroine and her reconquered lover helter-skelter along with the dead and the dying through the city decimated by plague, Bette Davis has no equal or emulator on the screen. Barely pretty, she contains the power to become beautiful in fits and starts whenever she wills it, giving the sensual passages a weight that is fleeting, surprising, and precise. In these moments, she reminds me of the one French actress who equals her in the freedom of her movement, the spontaneity of her perfect gestures, her walk, and her inflection—I'm referring to Valentine Tessier.

I hope that a movie theater in Paris will think of reviving *Jezebel*. Besides the audience, the artists of the cinema need to admire, to understand what Bette Davis is doing—violent with a muffled voice; majestic in her little girl's stature; emotional without letting a tear fall from her large, bulging eyes. Our nursery of stars, new and hardworking, have everything to learn. They will measure, in watching Bette Davis, what separates raw talent, disdainful of grandiloquence, from the reserve with which Garbo restrains herself, and disguises her timidity as well as her relative lack of power.

Garbo's subdued acting still influences a majority of women, in France or elsewhere. What Garbo did not dare, did know how to externalize, she limited herself—if I may say so—to stifling, relying for the rest on her noble beauty, her long beauty that fears being ruffled. The School of Garbo, the obsession with Garbo, paralyzes our wonderful young women, who have so far done nothing wondrous. Our film industry has for several years now made good movies and created bad female roles.

From Both Sides of the Curtain

This text is actually drawn from two lectures that Colette gave about her life in the theater. She delivered one lecture on February 8, 1924, and the other on November 15, 1924. Colette jokes about her thick accent from the province of Burgundy, which was a liability in French theater. She also mentions several figures from French drama. Georges Wague was a famous mime whom Colette performed with, notably in the play *La Chair [Flesh]*. Christine Kerf was an actress who also appeared frequently with Colette. Sacha Guitry (1885–1957) was an actor, director, playwright, and screenplay author who wrote more than 120 plays. The Tarride family boasted several actors, including Abel (1865–1951), Jean (1901–1980), and Jacques (1903–1994). Firmin Gémier (1869–1933) was a famous actor and director who created the title role in Alfred Jarry's play *Ubu Roi*. Colette refers in these lectures to a prank that actors play to make one of their troupe break out laughing on stage, called *corpsing* in the U.K., because it is sometimes done by having an actor secretly wink or grin while playing a corpse. Marguerite Moreno (1871–1948) was a renowned actress and close friend of Colette. The Fratellini are a circus family, so their makeup is exaggerated.

Theater now conducts itself in the world a bit like a little woman newly arrived in polite society who doesn't know how to sit down without making her skirt puff out too much.

At the time when I, as they say, strutted the boards, right away they treated me indulgently as a sort of foreigner without a future there. When I made my debut as a playwright, the critics didn't want to crush in one fell swoop and forever this eccentric who, no doubt, would not repeat the crime. So I benefited from the general indulgence that didn't imagine that this foreigner and this eccentric might come to them, not only as a foreigner, but as a "spy"; I would even say (although the word is too strong) almost as an enemy.

The first tableau [I acted in when I was learning to be a mime], featured a village festival. An unknown man, a stranger, walks down a mountain footpath, interrupts the farandole and the joyful dancing, while the peasants ask in sign language, "But, stranger, where are you from?" Which the poor boy was supposed to answer with hand gestures, "I'm from a faraway land where the young women, on Sunday evening, dance with red scarves wrapped around their hair buns!"

I don't know if I was just a hopeless novice, but I could never understand how one could express in gestures *Sunday evening* and even, *the red scarf*.

[The music hall] is where I surprised the magician at his trick; that's where I felt for the anguish of the trained animal; that's where I discovered the secret panting of the acrobat and the contortionist, of the snake-man whose contortions—even though he did them on a daily basis—still tortured him. That's where I happened to hear the well-concealed moans of the strong man, who one day caught his bronze canon slightly at an angle and on the nape of his neck, while smiling and waving to the audience, hid a wound that he had just received and which he was groaning from quietly. While you, you were applauding how graceful they looked, I, from the other side of the curtain, I took in the convulsive grimace, and the muttered blasphemy, and the strain masked for you. At that moment, I saw the glittering sprite who had just finished whirling and flying in front of you and me, return to the shadows behind the set, dragging two injured feet. It's at that moment that I saw, behind the set, all the color drain from the face of an adolescent, who in just a second on stage was about to hold out with a frail hand an ace of hearts as a target for a rifle, and I could hear on his chest the tinkling of charms and good-luck medallions because they were shaking so hard. And I saw the beautiful Hindu snake charmer change her costume, right next to me, with the innocence of a naked child. You, you saw them on stage, but, during this time, it was I who heard alone the rustling of oiled silk made by snakes waking in their crates.

It was during this time that one day, behind the set, a wolf that was also waiting his turn, reached his mouth between the bars of his cage and seized my hand as it was dangling down, and since he didn't clamp his jaws, I believe that on that evening he treated me as his friend, and as a fellow performer.

That was where I saw a beautiful classical dancer arriving from the other side of the curtain, and without taking the time to unlace any part of her costume, she ran to the dressing room where her infant, who was four months old, was waiting, lying in a compartment of a trunk; and I can still see that beautiful girl who nursed her infant in a dancer's pose, that is putting all her weight on one foot, with her skirts in a wheel around her, and I see the magnificent gesture that she made in pulling her beautiful breast out of her bodice to give it to her child. And she nursed the infant like that—all her weight on one foot, with her hands pulled back behind her—because she didn't want to touch the baby with her hands all full of makeup and so cold. It's one of the most noble images that I took away from my life in music halls.

It's there that I saw all sides of a self-enclosed and mysterious world; it's there that heroism is naive and joy is childlike.

For you, these memories are nothing but a passing image; for me, these images have taken on the power of a state of the soul. So here are some that I hope you will allow me to mention to you:

My friend Georges Wague, Christine Kerf, and I, we had to get on a night train. It was in a rainy town, and in bad weather. When you talk about a rainy town, you sometimes think of Saint-Étienne, but it wasn't necessarily Saint-Étienne. It was on a black night, in a rainy town. It was 12:30, after midnight, all the lights had been turned off, the show was over, and we were walking across the stage, carrying our luggage. The stage was dark and sliced only by a single beam because of the light they turn on at the front of the stage when the show is over, which they call "the ghost light." And in this darkness, on this stage, in this fairly sinister blackness, two Chinese people were repacking their luggage, like us, the diminutive and fragile luggage of prestidigitators, consisting of a few boxes, stacked together, artificial flowers, and their yellow faces expressed an incurable melancholy. They didn't speak a word, and all the light on the stage seemed to come, at that hour, from a flight of doves, trained doves who took their exercise like prisoners and who, under the roof of the theater, wheeled around and around and came to roost on the shoulders of the ones whom I called their tormentors, since nothing is sadder than the fate of the trained animal, especially when it's a dove. They alighted there tenderly, cooing. They were doves of the type that is pinkish white, with a little black necklace; then they whirled around the ceiling of the stage exactly like a flight of rose petals from a game of "she-loves-me, she-loves-me-not."

For you this is only a memory, a little optical memory. For me, this image has remained symbolic, melancholy, with no escape, of unassuaged tenderness, of resignation, so true is it that once you are marked for literature, literature insinuates itself perhaps into simplest of images, but I can't say that this image is only about literature.

[In this section, Colette recounts what happened when the author of a comic sketch objected to the way an actor said her line, "And now, I'm taking you all to the Pré Catelan." (one of Paris's fanciest restaurants, in the Bois de Boulogne).]

"No, honey, not like that! If you were going to take your friends after supper to the Pré Catelan, what would you say to them?"

"Well, I'd say, 'I'm taking you all to the Pré Catelan!'"

"That's it, honey, say it just like that!"

But she had a sense of decorum and a sense of the tradition of the variety show, so she fortunately reminded the author about how things really made sense by saying to him, "Oh, Monsieur Cottens, but on stage . . . !"

She knew that the variety show has its own tradition, she knew you had to ham it up—it was part of the tradition; it's art!

You laugh about all this quite nicely, and truly, it doesn't take that much to make you laugh, since these are things you haven't heard before, thank God!

I can't keep secret from you much longer that when it comes to the theater, I didn't have much success as an actress, either in Paris, or in the provinces. I can say now that Paris didn't understand me. No, Paris didn't understand me, and the drama critics, those awful drama critics who are now my colleagues, testified that I hadn't lost my Bungundian accent, that I rolled my *r*s when speaking; you are my witnesses, though, since you've heard me speak, that this is completely untrue and all that is obviously just a conspiracy!

But in the end, there had to be something more than that criticism, which was ultimately benign, to keep me in that world I didn't know: there was my incurable and untiring curiosity, the bewilderment and the stupor that I felt in getting to know, on that side of the curtain, a type of humanity that resembled in no way what I had left behind at the music hall.

I know well that in all eras the music hall and the theater have exchanged stars, and this has served the best interests of both the theater and the music hall. But the stars they exchange bring with them, so to speak, their bits of nudity or of stardom, they don't contribute to creating around them what I would call, not to use an ungracious term, but just to make myself clear, what I would call an atmosphere of constantly showing off. This strange world of actors, this world where professional solidarity is a magnificent thing, but where individual ferocity is no less magnificent and in a sense primeval, the glimpse I caught of it astonished me, and since that time, because I've stayed in touch with it, it never ceases to amaze me. Seen from that side of the curtain, the world of the theater is a mythical land where nerves become a focus of discussion as if they were an occult power or a company of elves.

It's a world where rivalries manifest themselves in all sorts of ways, and not only in the competition for parts, but also in the color of a dress worn on stage, or a jewel, or a carriage—in fact anything that can become a subject of rivalry. It's a world that sustains itself on pride, and even vanity, but it's also a world where pride in the profession comes first, in short, above pride plain and simple. It's a world, finally, which it must seem to you that I'm speaking about with an animosity so unjust that you can easily recognize a bitterness of the sort that follows great disappointment. Thank God, it's not quite that! I will never forget the modest debuts I made in the theater, I will never forget that I was well compensated with pleasure and fun. It's enough for my artistic vanity that I appeared in the cast, in a minuscule theater, of a comedy by Mr. Sacha Guitry called *Horsehair*.

Does anyone here remember *Horsehair*? No? There you go, you've forgotten me already! Impossible!

It was a sweet little play where its very young author—very young at the time, since I'm speaking of about fourteen to fifteen years ago—where its very young author had already incorporated his well-known humor and young man's imagination into the plot. In fact, the play had all it needed, except the seven or eight last lines that came right before the final curtain. We had all of one week to get the play ready, and every day we protested to the author that we needed the end of *Horsehair*, the last strands of this horse's hair. Each time he promised us we would have it the very next day. In the end, on the day of the final afternoon rehearsal, before the final dress rehearsal that night, we still didn't have the final lines, so we were waiting for the author who was supposed to bring them to the afternoon rehearsal. We waited for him for an hour, an hour and a half, and more. Finally, at five p.m., the director rushed away in a taxi, we were all in a mad panic, and he came back an hour later and transmitted the answer that was given to him by a black servant: Monsieur Sacha Guitry had left that very morning for a two-month-long trip to Holland!

You can imagine the deflation of the morale of the actors, poor actors that we were! We did what we could, we inserted what they call action, we added jokes, we even added a bit of dance, we included humor, even a spritz of a seltzer bottle that I pointed with sure hands in the direction of the orchestra seats. Obviously that was all very nice, but it wasn't the same as the few lines that the author was supposed to add to *Horsehair*. But it wasn't because of this that fourteen days after the first performance, the manager of this minuscule theater ran off with the box office proceeds, and at the same time, our salaries, which were just as minuscule.

I experienced a sharp sense of disappointment from a financial standpoint, but do you think I lost my sense of humor and my curiosity? No, you don't know me if you said that. I gained, on the contrary, a sudden sense of confidence in my gifts, since that accident resulted in my suddenly being anointed as an actor. I was mistaken. Experience showed that. But I consulted the experts, I resolved to work hard, and I went to get advice from Tarride.

Tarride was very sweet. How could Tarride not be sweet? He's a delightful boy. He listened to me with much kindness, and he said to me, "Don't you think, that of all the arts, you'd be best suited for pantomime?"

I didn't want to contradict Tarride, so I went to see Gémier. Gémier was also charming. How could Gémier not be charming? He said to me, "What in the world was that dance you did out there on stage? I'm telling you, what you need is some good choreography!"

Armed with these excellent suggestions, I went to see my friend and teacher, Christine Kerf, to inform her that I would become a dancer. She got straight to the point, with that trace of a Flemish accent that drifts back into her voice sometimes and that I find delicious: "Yo, yo, yo, what in the world are you thinking! Listen, you're not young enough to start dance. Do you think you can start dance seriously at your age? You have to start very young! You don't even know how to do a jump. Dance isn't going to work for you."

Thus encouraged, I didn't lose my equanimity, nor that untiring curiosity that got me from wing to wing, from dressing room to dressing room, from the fireman's stall to the prompter's box, and from stage to stage, until—I didn't foresee this!—I ended up in a puppet show, where the author of the drama, in front of the stage, surveys his play, and his own play comes into being, patiently taking shape.

At times there is definitely a sort of courage in literature, pared down to its basics: you pit yourself against a blank page, with a character you have just created and who, nevertheless, already governs in her own way her own life in the novel, and imposes on your brain her ghostly vitality, the whimsy of a specter born in the moonlight. Obviously, there is a sort of prideful pleasure in a duel of wits with this creature from your brain who already has a will, in the triumph over her. But what is the equivalent of this great pleasure when it comes to theater? Because to knead for the stage, on the stage, living beings, speaking beings, mulish or docile, ungrateful or magnificent, perfectible or incurable, what attracts you, I repeat, what binds you to the theater, is this prideful pleasure. It consists in saying to an actor or an actress, in a rehearsal:

> There you are, with your grayish-greenish suit, or maybe your threadbare jacket, there you are with your fifty years, there you are with your impoverished hair, with your dyed hair, your rheumatism! Still, you will be the irresistible young man, you will be the virgin in the springtime of her life, you will be a courtesan with no bounds, you will be a mother torn apart, and it will be my fault, and it will be my work, and I will knead you with my own hands, and you will rehearse one hundred times your attempt to make yourself cry spontaneously, your attempt at crystalline laughter, your drunken faint, you will rehearse as many times as I like until I'm content and until I tell you, "That's good—now do it better."

That is the true attraction of the theater, and it's an admirable duty, backbreaking rehearsals, it's a satisfaction that's intense and yet never exhausted that theater offers to our instincts of a little Nero of the republic. I have tasted that autocracy, and I assure you, the way it binds you to the theater is much more dangerous than success!

You've seen that childish and juvenile infectious laughter on the stage that seizes one actor and then spreads to another and then another. Every actor at one time or another becomes the target of a conspiracy: we're going to make her laugh, and we'll get her, they say, we'll get her before the end of the play. This conspiracy spread and went as high as Sarah Bernhardt herself. She was acting, at this time, in *The Witch* by Sardou. Pretty much everyone, I think, wanted more or less surreptitiously to make the great Sarah laugh on stage, but Sarah, with the equilibrium that she was famous for, with her willpower, was too dominant, there was nothing that could make Sarah burst out laughing on stage. She was completely in her art and didn't hear anything else. Nevertheless, in the scene of the Tribunal of the Inquisition, she couldn't hold out.

I'm going to set the scene a little. On one side, the Tribunal of the Inquisition; on the other side, the judges are presiding over our dear De Max; on the ground, supplicating, prostrate before them, holding up her beautiful white arms, a perfectly innocent witch who is none other than Sarah herself. A witness for the prosecution enters on this side: Marguerite Moreno, madeup as a witch: hooked nose, black, in rags, supported by a stick, in short, the traditional witch—oh, so evil!

One night, Marguerite Moreno enters from that side of the stage. She had made up the right side of her face the way she usually did, as an old witch, with wrinkles, with charcoaled eyebrows. But on the other side, from her nose to the line of her chin, had made herself up in a way that would not have disappointed a Fratellini clown. She has an eyebrow up on her forehead; a red and drippy eye on her cheek; and, even worse, she has a wart in modeling dough with horsehair growing out of it. She enters the set, and the audience can't see a thing. But the Tribunal of the Inquisition, who are facing that side of her, start to be sick with laughter. The judges lose their composure and De Max is having a hard time keeping a straight face. Sarah, who is on the ground imploring the Tribunal, sees perfectly well that the infectious laughter is winning out, and between the lines of her part she hammers out these words: "You will all be punished, you will all be punished! Infamy! Disgusting!" She continues with her role, but things do not improve with the Tribunal, just the opposite. Finally, since it's in the script, Sarah turns toward the awful witch to say to her: "But tell me, miserable witch . . ." And turning around she catches sight of Marguerite Moreno. That night they got Sarah Bernhardt, and they got her so good that instead of saying, "Miserable witch," she repeated three times in a loud and clearly audible voice—and you know how her voice could carry—"Miserable Moreno! Miserable Moreno! Miserable Moreno!"

I think they lowered the curtain, but if I add this, it's not because it's true, but just to have a good ending for my story.

The modern stage can no longer, without peril, use highly literary vocabulary or noble syntax.

Because if modern theater, modern comedy, modern tragedy does follow or should follow real life, there are no longer—if there ever were—heroes or heroines who can use without impunity noble French and classical oratory. Theater cannot escape its own time. If it's the time of loose-fitting dresses, the time of short hair, the time of slightly more brutish morals, a little more relaxed than they were in former times, it's obvious that if you put on stage in a modern comedy a father shaved in the American style and wearing a jacket with a half-belt for his morning sports, if you put him together with his daughter with her closely cropped hair and in a dress made from two and a half yards of fabric, and in a narrow width to boot, a dress that has no sleeves, collar, or flounce, which has nothing at all, and if you put in the mouths of these two characters, for example, this dialogue that I collected from a slightly old-fashioned play, but which is neither melodrama nor inflated prose (it's about a marriage proposal, of course, since this is the first act):

"Approach, my daughter. I summoned you here expressly to communicate to you a project that is the culmination of all my wishes and which, I hope, will also serve your own. The Viscount des Granges, this very morning, has come to me to ask for your hand."

"Oh, father!" answers the young woman, "You see I am as moved as I am happy! The Viscount des Granges is among those to whom a young woman may safety entrust her destiny, or so I believe. Before you, my father, I will join my hand to that of Hubert des Granges."

All this is perfectly proper, it's not even extremely bombastic, except—I don't know if you share my opinion here—it's completely impossible now! Just as there are now limits on stage to impropriety, there are also now limits on stage to high style, and, without going so far as to respond, as not a few young women would do when asked the same question: "No problem, Dad!" obviously the young woman of today finds herself obliged to lower the tone and to keep a note of contemporary truth, and we begin, we the audience (I'm crossing over to the other side of the curtain, I'm rejoining the audience!) are beginning only to be moved, and to believe that the young woman and her father exist in real life, at the moment when they begin to speak more or less the same way we do, that is, very badly.

I struggled with my utter presumptuousness, since I was completely new to this profession, so much so that I knew nothing about it. I arrived with what they call "a fresh eye," and I struggled, for instance, against the craze for the handkerchief in the palm of the hand that the young woman madly in love brings into the first act, and clutches until the end of the third act. I tried to struggle against the fingers hooked into the vest, or the hands in pants pockets, which assure composure in difficult moments for the young lead or the young supporting actor; against the floppy shrugs of the ingenue; and also against the gesture that I saw the ingenue reverting to, which is somewhat comical and nervous, and which is fairly new, which I've noticed on certain stages and which consists in crooking a finger under the nose because it makes her look like a good girl, and natural. I struggled against all that, all that and many other things, with utter presumptuousness, with unheard of self-possession. When you're an actor without talent, you can't imagine how much you know about what the other actors, those *with* talent, should be doing or not doing.

After weeks of journeyman acting, of work, weeks of discussions, weeks of bitterness, weeks of lyricism and bursts of enthusiasm, suddenly, since it was a quarter to nine, I ended up entirely alone, there on the other side of the stage, in a little space called the production department, where they store broken lamps and furniture with three legs. I found myself in a solitude where I could no longer hear the sounds of everyday life; the daily work was gone, and so were those whom I had lived with so closely— they had all suddenly left me. And I was alone because the actors were practicing their profession, they were performing the play. The director, whom we had had words with during the rehearsals, was also going about his business, in the stage box to the right, and my collaborator, he, too, had gone. He was everywhere, he was in the box office, he was doing what I should've been doing, in short. I was utterly alone, and this solitude took a form so bitter, so emotional, that truly, instead of emotion, instead of the type of joy, of nervousness that is all I should've felt when thinking about the outcome of that dress rehearsal, suddenly I felt like a person completely alone, completely abandoned, above all someone nobody needed anymore at all. I was there, alone, with an azalea plant that hadn't found a spot in the dressing room of the artist it had been sent to—always red azaleas in those situations—I was there, with that azalea plant beginning to wilt, in a state of solitude that was unfathomable and bitter beyond measure. There was nothing funny about it. It was a sensation that caused me more pain than I should permit myself.

After some time had passed, I heard a sort of noise, a weak and distant lapping. I didn't recognize it because I had never heard it before from this location, and after that, another noise, noises of voices, this time voices I knew, and then all the actors came in, I saw my previous life come storming back, I witnessed such a warm onrush, so much affection, so filled with excited talk, with the arms of friends, with rouged mouths, lively faces, even friends, who came from the audience, also enemies, all of that flooded me so with that warmth that I was lacking that I suddenly felt myself turning pale emotionally—I felt a shock, a shock that struck so close to my heart that I said to myself:

How can it be that these actors—all these people whom I've only known for three or four weeks—I already love them so much, how can it be that they have become so necessary to me? My God! How I've been bitten, how deeply the poison of the theater has already seeped into my blood, how much I need them, how much I feel that it will be vital, one way or another, to find them again, either them or others! And I can clearly see, I admit, that there is only one way to find them again, to feel their warmth again, their sharp hunger for living that they have passed on to me, there is only one way, and I'm going to do it right away—I'm not going to resist any longer. I'm going to write another play!

A Distinguished Connoisseur

At the time when this piece takes place, Colette was performing opposite the famous mime, Georges Wague, in the notorious drama *Flesh*. It was in this play that Colette became famous for baring her breasts on stage, although that does not figure in her story, which is about a claque. Traditionally in the theater, a claque was a group of people hired to sit in the audience and applaud loudly in order to stimulate the crowd to respond enthusiastically to the performance. First published in *Le Nouveau Siècle* on December 5, 1909.

I was appearing in *Flesh*, so I had to change trains in . . . let's see, is it the second or third largest city in France? Doesn't matter. The second, the third, and the fourth largest city in France all have their "first-class establishment" where you can rake in "a nice take of three thousand five." So you settle for the three thousand five. Now I know that in almost all these first-class establishments—Kursaal-Casino, Casino-Kursaal, Eldorado, Eden-Concert—you will find, at the bottom of a staircase that smells of cabbage, a dressing room where you can smell the latrine; and the same slop pail, so small, but so dirty!

My friend Wague, the skilled mime, is putting on his costume in the dressing room next to mine, and with our doors open, we chat. Wague, an old trooper, tries to pump me up as best he can, because I'm as sad as a caged animal, out of my element in this new cage: between us is born a nervous politeness, the fleeting effusiveness of exiles:

"So, Colette, did you see the marquee?"

"N . . . yes."

"Not bad, huh?"

"Yeah."

"It's the color of red currant syrup. And letters this big! When they give me letters so damn big, I wish my name was Nebuchad-nezzar, so it would be longer! The posters are nothing to sneeze at either, huh?"

"Yeah."

"And have you seen the toilets here?"

"No."

"Not so fun. I don't know how they managed it, but they're worse than Toulon."

"!!!"

"You can sigh all you want, but that's how it is. You remem-ber the ones in Toulon where somebody had written: *Here you strain to leave your rocks/Even the guys who work on the docks.* We had a really good laugh that day, didn't we?"

"Yeah."

"Y'know, the box office is pretty good here, today. I wouldn't mind coming back to this one-horse town. What about you?"

"Yeah."

" 'Yes,' 'No.' You're acting like you don't give a flying f . . . , you know that? Lucky for you I'm here. Who else worries about the posters, the photos for the program, the train schedules, every-thing! It's me, the lover boy, because, if it was up to you . . ."

"I know."

"Like for the claque, if I wasn't here. . . . I talked to the head of the claque just now. Very refined. An intelligent guy, distin-guished. He looks like an executive in some office. He'll warm things up discretely. He has tact. I spotted that right away. Listen, someone's ringing."

"Is it for us?"

"No, my mistake. First there's the jumping dogs, then the number with the Chilean acrobats. We're after that."

Midnight. Same location, after the show. Flushed, nervous, wired by the dancing and the applause, I sing in my dressing room while I take off my makeup, and the inexplicable silence of my friend Wague, in the dressing room next to mine, is getting on my nerves. But his precise motivation, his clear expressions and gestures, his final suicide all went over well, as usual.

"Hey, Wague, what a house, huh?"

"—"

"How about that, pal—four curtain calls!"

"Uh huh."

"That's not enough for you? What did you take tonight? Let me get a word in edgewise, will you? What's the matter?"

Wague's face, ferocious, smeared with Vaseline and thinned out ochre and blue, appears: "What's the *matter*? You have the nerve to ask me what's the matter?"

"Well . . . yeah!"

He burst out: "What's the matter? The claque. Did you hear the claque?"

"No, but since the audience spontaneously . . ."

"They didn't make a single peep, the claque. Did you see those guys, that line of pimps, idiots, nitwits, clods, just sitting up there like a shelf of cheeses? Did you see him, that old geezer?"

"The head of the claque? The man with the distinguished air? The one who looks like an executive?"

Wague shakes his shoulders frenetically: "Him? An executive? You want me to tell you what he looks like, with his hair plastered on his head? Like a rat who fell in sh-t! Anyway, I'm waiting for him right now, and we'll see why his regiment of sausages didn't march!"

My friend Wague didn't have to wait long. The "executive" turned up, perky, imperious, and supremely distinguished.

"So, *there* you are!" Wague shouted.

"Yes, here I am," conceded this superior man. "I imagine you're pleased."

"Pleased? Pleased? Are you f-ing kidding me? Who told your guys to sit on their hands right when the dance started, and then just when the dress is pulled off, and then right in the knife scene when the blood spurts out? Huh, who was it?"

The "executive," with a hand in a worn-out kid glove, waves away these reproaches as if they were bothersome flies. His thick, old woman's face grimaces, with all its pretentious folds. And as soon as he can get in a word, he defends himself, exasperated, but courteous: "Monsieur, monsieur, if you please! I have tact, and what's more, I know my profession. What is a claque? Can you tell me what a claque is?"

"—"

"Then permit me, sir. The claque is a coarse tonic, intended for anemic numbers. It is a vulgar spice that seasons a hysterical dance, it's . . ."

"It's a f-ing waste of a gold louis!" Wague interrupts bitterly.

"Permit me, monsieur! This tonic, this spice, I lavish them on those who need it, do you understand? *Those who need it!* But artists such as yourself, monsieur, and madame! I would blush, as a man of tact who knows his profession, to underline, to bruise what you do. Do you know what you do? What you do is beautiful! And beauty can't be bought, not for a louis, not for even one hundred francs, monsieur! I bow before beauty, but I never interfere with it!"

French Wine, Perfumes, and Dolls

The Wines of France

This essay by Colette was first published as a promotional piece in 1935 by the celebrated wine merchant Nicolas and Company. It was written at a time when cocktails and martinis where beginning to replace wine as a popular drink. *Yquem* refers to the wines of the Château d'Yquem in the Graves region of southern Bordeaux. The white wines of this region have a deep golden color.

Madame Achille Fould
will be at home
on Saturday, June the Second
from 6 to 8 p.m.
92, Avenue Henri-Martin

If Madame Fould had consulted me first, I would have suggested the following text:

"Madame Fould and the Wines of France will be at home, from six to eight p.m., Avenue Henri-Martin."

The audacious hostess preferred to strike out in red the word "cocktail." Now we know that in France red is the color of revolution, and this one gesture from her authoritative hand knocks the usurper off its pedestal, promotes to the throne the legitimate sovereign recalled from exile, who returns jovially and with his head free, happy, and not reeling, his complexion florid and his heart solid: His Royal Highness, The Wine.

Madame Achille is not just trying to stage a coup, she's attempting a coup de grâce: she has to succeed. Her method is the best. She's chosen for her knights all those who love wine, and behind them trail the sizeable avant-garde of snobs.

Since my childhood I've known French wine and spoken to it as a familiar. At the age when a child's thirst is slaked, at snack time or dessert, by black currant syrup mixed with bubbly mineral water, I held in one hand my pretty little tulip-shaped glass, glowing red with a Bordeaux at room temperature, redolent of violets, unless it was illuminated by a slightly oily Yquem that shone like topaz. With the other hand I balanced, from glass to mouth and from mouth to glass, one of those "dunking cookies" that made you, as we said in the region where I was born, "hungry to drink." They are distant now, my oenophile childhood and youth. Where are those ladyfinger cookies, pleasant accomplices of the wine?

Thick, stubby sponge cakes, four to a row, held together by a fragile membrane, cookies that seemed hard as stone but weakened, melted, in contact with wine? Pink cookies, with a hint of vanilla, destined for vintage reds, and excellent cookies made in Montbozon, now impossible to find . . . Created for wine, they followed it and recoiled, faced with an invasion of undrinkable drinks, petroleums, ethers, liquors that could polish copper, mixtures invented by this insane craze for cocktails. They will return, I hope, with wine at nightfall, with walnuts and cheese that enliven old wine, chestnuts with their weakness for first-year wines, tartines with anchovies that keep their Provençal accent. And those thick, savory, round galettes that I'd forgotten! The latter, my close friends know that I reserve for mulled wine, the great exorcist of winter crepuscules that fall as early as three o'clock.

Would you prefer a cup of tea? You can have it! After a long and sober work day, I'll stick with my little carafe of Beaujolais well heated, with a cinnamon stick swimming right in its mauve froth. Around the brown, earthenware pot spreads an aroma of nutmeg and lemon, barely perceptible, since heated wine cringes at strong spices. Palates are moistened and tongues are unfettered, which is not the smallest miracle of the Wine of France—whether it's cool or hot, fluid and pearled with bubbles, or unctuous and sticking slightly to the sides of the crystal—it resuscitates French conversation.

French conversation has come a long way. Like swallows that were not able to emigrate in winter, it lived a petty and precarious existence. Sleep, alcohol, death, all threatened it. Thanks to Wine, it reawakened, aided by subjects as ancient as the vines themselves. It sings of Wine in beautiful words: bouquet, legs, roundness, velvet. It speaks of Wine as if discussing a living being, probes its past and banks on its future, sees it grow and descend along hills planted with stakes. When a hand is raised, brandishing the captive glow that evokes gold, dawn, the reddish and sumptuous end of the day, when a voice enthusiastically affirms, "Now this wine, guys, this is a somebody!" I smile at Wine crowned with hyperbole, engenderer of poems, Wine that reclaims among humankind its familiar and magnificent allegorical figure.

Fragrances

This piece was written as a promotional pamphlet, issued as a booklet by Lanvin perfumes in 1949. Passy is a fashionable neighborhood on the Right Bank of Paris in the 16th Arrondissement, on the west side of the city. Madame de Mortsauf is a character in Honoré de Balzac's novel *The Lily of the Valley*. Colette also mentions Maréchale perfume, a short name for Eau à la Maréchale, a famous scent created in 1669 for the Maréchale d'Aumont, wife of Maréchal [Marshal] d'Aumont.

Back then, in Passy, in an empty lot, there was . . .

What was there, actually? Nothing discernable except a scent. But such a scent! My young nose, more acute than it is now, found pretexts—I even went so far as to pay frequent visits my first mother-in-law in the 16th Arrondissement—just to arrive at the point where the rue Singer meets the rue des Vignes, that point, invisible and precise, from which the scent arose. First a bit fruity, then revealing a reseda that the slightest wind would disperse . . . but what authority can pinpoint exactly the perfume of the reseda—is it the flower, on those little yellow puffs without much character? Reseda was the perfume of a particular era. A slender thread linked it to the violet, and both of them together lost their weak redolence, which our mothers all considered extremely distinguished.

But in this empty lot no tangible reseda contributed to make up the scent of Passy; no actual heliotrope intervened, as a mysterious fourth agent, when I leaned my elbows on the disjointed picket fence.

As entertainment, also as an affliction of the most noble of our senses, the search for a perfume can only be an obsession. My stops when I leaned against the fence, nostrils open above the waste and the glass shards, resulted by chance in this clarification: a nearby maker of jams was crushing black currants and was accumulating the residue, not completely bloodless, in a corner of the enclosure. A gardener, their neighbor, was doing the same for his slightly putrefied bulbs of the lily variety that had lost their flowers. A few of the remains, no doubt touched by a downpour, and relying on a small miracle of fermentation, accounted for the rest, creating that brief moment while the odoriferous must of the recently pressed grapes still murmured in the vat.

As with all olfactory wonders, this one that preoccupied me ceased as soon as the particles that had engendered it suffered a new death, and I followed other surprises, led by my nose, which has always guided me to the best and the worst. More dependent on chance encounters than on research, often I've found myself surrounded, stopped in the center of the universe that a fragrance opens, then closes, a fragrance less explicit than those sweet, those floral odors, those smells proclaimed by foliage that holds no secrets: "Hi, I'm mint!" "I'm the melissa balm that bees love!" "I'm the pelargonium that masks all the impertinence of a Mediterranean climate." It's not that simple, the whiff that carries to our nostrils what I call enchanting fetidness. Issuing from decomposed wood and from its nocturnal phosphorescence, it also depends on the fleeting mushroom, on the silt of a delicately musked stream, since the stream has slid over the dry leather of a little frog, tanned by its remote death. Lean forward: rising toward us is the fine odor that doesn't dare tell its name, the paradisial scent that wafted around Saint Lidwina of Schiedam, blessed one whose wounds and body released balmy aromas after her death.

Balzac said . . . but what didn't he say? He is, for his fervent fans, of which I am one, an inexhaustible jungle. He touched on everything, even perfumes. His flaring nostril drank them in. He spoke of vernal grass, the tender shoot that is the soul of "mown hay." He celebrated the black and pink fumitory, which smells a bit like soot if you crush it; the large scarlet poppy and its teardrops of opium; the aggressive rest-harrow that flowers like a sweaty blonde. But if he had sung the praises of only the rose and the lily of the valley, I would not be such a loyal fan. The sheaf he assembles at the feet of Madame de Mortsauf doesn't even equal in its arrangement and colors the bouquet of a country bride. But does that matter? That little impetuous man had a sense of smell like a wildcat. When he sniffs, I no longer dare to doubt the rumor that a man's nostril is more expert than ours, although mine doesn't fear many rivals. The fact is that modern industry values their wine tasters and the chemists of perfumeries, and that their laboratories do not like the presence of women with their lunar disturbances. But it's for the woman that they labor, so she has the last word.

I've had the time to get to know various fashions in perfumes, to come to prefer the "Maréchale" scents over the corylopsis. A passing brutality, during the last war, saturated women with essences that seemed to rely on a brutal pharmacopoeia, awful perfumes that I wanted to call "Beats You with a Stick," or "Bull

Killer," or "Industrial Strength." More than once I surrendered my seat to them, at a restaurant where they robbed me of my appetite, or at the theater where they distracted me from the play. Fortunately, bad taste never reigns too long in France. An art as French as deluxe perfume touches perfection these days. Dress and bottle, eager to wear the same brand, join together, resemble one another. The expensive phial takes on a slim waistline, the dress is shapely. Sure of being recognized everywhere, they sally forth, travel the seas, and the antipodes witness their double triumph.

Ðolls

For many years Colette had a vacation house in the French province of Brittany. In this personal essay, Colette celebrates the renowned maker of dolls from Brittany, Madame Le Minor (1901–1984). Mathurin Méheut (1882–1958) was an artist who popularized the landscapes and customs of Brittany in his work, and influenced the doll maker. Koua-nin is a Daoist deity. First published in *Revue française de l'élite*, number 9, 1948.

I wasn't the type who played with dolls in those days. It was my half-sister, the older one, when she was twenty, twenty-four years old. When she was twenty-four she got married, and that was a mistake—she was much happier in her pretty room of an adolescent girl, amidst the childish and feminine disorder of the dolls she dressed up in such good taste. She said that her three dolls—Bee, Isabelle, and Alice—belonged to me, but I didn't like them. I admired not the toys but my half-sister's fine work, not the imitations of children they give to children, but the complete miniature trousseau, the skirting that you could finger like the tufts of a rose, the little tarlatan bloomers with the full skirt, over the little petticoat and the larger petticoat, the latter embroidered with lace, the former scalloped. There were even stockings, fashioned out of an old stocking; and shoes, cut from the cuffs of a suede glove.

I admired them, but I didn't possess them. Possession—a marvelous, brutal, and complete education, uses touch in tandem with sight and the imagination, and chooses its moment. I waited quite a long time to dare to play with dolls, that is, to allow next to my fireplace, despite their various persuasions, the stiff Koua-nin of yellow amber, a little wooden Madonna that the eighteenth century imprinted with graceful frivolity, a Dahomeyan fetish with a chicken's beak, and my dolls from Brittany.

This will not surprise any devotee of Brittany—not to confuse devotion with expertise—to say that the latter have the most vibrant color, the richest gold and silver thread, the best decorative braid. But here the imagination plays no part, it's tradition that guides the hand of Madame Le Minor, the great dressmaker of dolls from Brittany.

Another art of superior quality is that of Mathurin Méheut— whoever guides her would not compromise with truth or science. This unknown treasure, who seems to belong to an ancient civilization, and to follow decorative laws whose origins are now lost, Méheut makes himself their guardian and trustee.

I came to dolls as art objects through Madame Le Minor. But it's through Méheut—who made such a beautiful album of full color images for a text of mine—that I fell hopelessly in love with the seas of Brittany. Without reducing itself to the narrow viewpoint of documentation, Méheut's sweeping seascapes make no errors with regard to a ship's gear or masts, and believe only him if you want to find on the chest of someone from Brittany, on the day of their traditional penitential pilgrimage, the likeness of an embroidery from Armorica, or Coptic palm leaves preserved through the centuries. I don't demand that much from a painter in the way of documentary science; I'm content if he gives me a faithful portrait of a dreamy and maleficent octopus; a gurnard leaning on its wattle; a serpentine bouquet of barnacles; and blooming along a path that leads inevitably to the sea, those skirts of Brittany, those aprons of Brittany, those farthingales worn by infantas, stiff silks that, passed down from mother to daughter, put to shame the paucity of today's textiles; opulent yards of black velvet, flowery ribbons, coiffes and bonnets, a panoply of millenary luxury inspired by the Orient that a whole province of France preserves; and that two French artists, with brush and needle, venerate.